IRELAND LORELEI

Jamaican Me Crazy Mon

A Vegabond Series Book

Contents

Note to Readers

The characters in this book are unapologetic and dramatic. The scenes are steamy and the road to happily ever after maybe twisted. This book is meant for audiences 18 years old and older. A list of potential triggering themes can be found on my website at https://irelandlorelei.com/possible-triggers

If you find any errors, I would like to hear about them. Please screenshot the page and email then to me at ireland@ireland-lorelei.com

Keisha's Burnout

The sound of sirens reverberated through the night, cutting through the thick, heavy air. With each passing moment, the cries of the emergency vehicles grew more persistent, as if the sirens were pleading with me to pay attention. But my heart wasn't in it. I had spent a year chasing after the elusive flames that licked the buildings of Miami, all while trying to unravel the twisted minds that set them alight. And now, I was completely and utterly spent.

The fire station loomed before me, its red brick exterior awash in the glow of streetlights. It was a bastion of safety, a sanctuary against the flames that threatened to consume the city. Yet, standing there on the sidewalk, I felt a sense of dread creeping in like a thief in the night. I knew that my time was running out, and that I needed to make a decision soon. But how could I walk away when there was so much left unresolved?

My name is Keisha Harper, and I am a journalist for the Miami Sentinel. For the past year, I have been investigating a series of arson cases alongside the city's fire department.

At first, the challenge of uncovering the truth behind these mysterious fires had been exhilarating. But as the days turned into weeks, and the weeks into months, the weight of my responsibility had become too much to bear.

For months, I had been running on fumes, subsisting on a diet of caffeine and adrenaline. My days were a blur of fire scenes, interviews, and frantic writing sessions, all while trying to maintain a semblance of a normal life outside of work. But the stress of the job was beginning to take its toll, and I knew that something had to give.

I could feel the strain on my relationships, as friends and family grew increasingly frustrated with my constant absence. But the one person who seemed to understand was my editor, Carla Martinez. She had been a mentor to me ever since I joined the Miami Sentinel, always offering her guidance and support. And in my darkest moments, she had been the one to remind me of the importance of our work.

"You're doing something important here, Keisha," she would tell me, her voice filled with conviction. "You're shedding light on a dark corner of the city, and giving a voice to those who have been silenced by fear. Don't give up, no matter how hard it gets."

But now, as I stood before the fire station, I couldn't help but feel that I had reached my breaking point. The adrenaline that had once fueled my passion for the job had long since drained away, leaving me hollow and empty inside. I felt like a burnt-out shell of my former self, my mind and body struggling to keep up with the demands of my work.

It wasn't just the physical exhaustion that was wearing me down, but the emotional toll as well. I had seen things that I could never forget, images that haunted my dreams and left me feeling as if I were wading through a sea of despair. And with each new case, I felt a growing sense of futility. No matter how many fires we extinguished, it seemed as if the flames would never truly be snuffed out.

The door to the fire station swung open, and a group of firefighters emerged, their faces grim and soot-streaked. As they passed by, I caught a glimpse of their haunted expressions, and I knew that I was not alone in my suffering. These brave men and women faced the same demons that I did, risking their lives every day to keep the city safe from the ravages of fire.

As I watched them trudge wearily towards their vehicles, I felt a sudden wave of resolve wash over me. I couldn't abandon them now, not when they needed me the most. It was true that I was tired, and that my spirit was flagging under the weight of my responsibilities. But if these firefighters could find the strength to carry on in the face of such adversity, then so could I.

I took a deep breath, letting the crisp night air fill my lungs and chase away the lingering traces of doubt and fear. I reminded myself that I was not just a journalist, but a guardian of truth, shining a light on the darkness that threatened to consume the city. And as long as there were fires to fight, I would be there, pen in hand, ready to document the battle.

With renewed determination, I strode into the fire station, the warmth of the building enveloping me like a comforting embrace. The familiar scent of smoke and sweat filled my nostrils, reminding me that this was where I belonged. This was my purpose, my calling, and I would not let burnout extinguish the flames of my passion.

As I made my way through the station, I could feel the curious eyes of the firefighters upon me. I knew that they respected me for the work I had done, and that they saw me as a kindred spirit, fighting the same battle that they did. And in their eyes, I saw the unspoken promise that they would stand by me, just as I had stood by them.

I reached the office of the fire chief, pausing for a moment to gather my thoughts. I knew that I needed to be honest with him about my struggles, and to seek his guidance in finding a way to overcome my burnout. As I raised my hand to knock on the door, I felt a flicker of hope begin to kindle within me, a spark that might one day grow into a roaring blaze.

And as I stepped into the fire chief's office, I vowed to myself that I would not let my burnout consume me. I would rise from the ashes, stronger and more determined than ever before. I would continue to fight the fires that threatened the city, and to bring the arsonists to justice.

For I was Keisha Harper, journalist and fire chaser, and I would not be defeated.

I stood there for a moment, taking in the familiar surroundings of the fire chief's office. The walls were lined with memorabilia and awards, a testament to his many years of service to the city. A map of Miami adorned one wall, red pins marking the sites of recent fires. The chief's desk was a monument to organized chaos, with stacks of paperwork and an assortment of firefighting paraphernalia.

As I approached the desk, Fire Chief Donovan looked up from the documents he was scrutinizing, his furrowed brow momentarily easing as he saw me. "Keisha," he said, his gruff voice betraying a hint of warmth. "What brings you here this late?"

I hesitated for a moment, unsure of how to begin. But as I met his steady gaze, I found the courage to speak my truth.

"Chief, I need to talk to you about something important," I said, my voice wavering slightly. "I think I might be…burning out."

He studied me for a moment, his eyes searching mine for any sign of insincerity. But as he saw the exhaustion etched into my features, his expression softened. "Sit down, Keisha," he said gently, gesturing to a chair across from his desk. "Let's talk."

As I sank into the worn leather seat, I suddenly found myself at a loss for words. How could I possibly convey the depth of my fatigue, the sense of hopelessness that had come to pervade my every waking moment? But as I looked into the chief's understanding eyes, I knew that I had to try.

For the next several hours, I poured out my heart to Chief Donovan, recounting the endless days and nights spent chasing after the arsonists that plagued our city. I told him about the dreams that haunted my sleep, nightmares filled with smoke and flames that left me drenched in sweat. And I shared my growing sense of despair, the feeling that no matter how many fires we put out, there would always be another one waiting just around the corner.

To his credit, Chief Donovan listened patiently, his face a mask of stoic concern. He did not interrupt or try to downplay my feelings, but simply let me speak my truth. And when I had finally finished, he leaned back in his chair, his gaze distant and thoughtful.

"Keisha," he began, his voice gentle but firm, "I want you to know that what you're feeling is completely normal. Burnout is a very real and very serious problem, especially in high-stress professions like ours. But that doesn't mean you're weak or that you're not cut out for this job. It just means that you're human, and that you need to find a way to recharge your batteries."

I nodded, grateful for his understanding. But I couldn't help but wonder if it was really possible for me to recover from my burnout. How could I possibly find the strength to carry on when it felt as if every ounce of my energy had been drained away?

Chief Donovan must have sensed my doubts because he continued, "I've seen many firefighters go through burnout over the years, Keisha. And I've learned that the key to overcoming it is to find a balance between your work and your personal life. You need to make time for yourself, to do the things that bring you joy and help you to relax."

I thought about his words, realizing that he was right. In my quest to bring the arsonists to justice, I had completely neglected my own well-being. My life had become a never-ending cycle of work, with little room for the hobbies and relationships that had once brought me happiness.

"But how do I find that balance, Chief?" I asked, my voice ting ed with desperation. "How do I manage to give my all to this job while still making time for myself?"

Chief Donovan leaned forward, resting his elbows on the desk. "It won't be easy, Keisha, but it's necessary. Start by setting boundaries. Allocate a certain number of hours each day for work and stick to it. When you're off the clock, make an effort to truly disconnect – no checking emails or messages related to work."

He paused, letting his advice sink in before continuing. "Next, prioritize self-care. Make sure you're eating well, getting enough sleep, and exercising regularly. These may seem like small things, but they can make a huge difference in your overall well-being."

I nodded, realizing that my neglect of these basic necessities had undoubtedly contributed to my burnout. It was time for me to start taking better care of myself, both physically and mentally.

"Finally," Chief Donovan said, "focus on rebuilding your relationships. Reach out to your friends and family, and make an effort to spend quality time with them. They are your support system, and they will help you through this difficult time."

Tears welled up in my eyes as I thought about the loved ones I had pushed away in my single-minded pursuit of the arsonists. I knew that I needed to make amends and rebuild those bridges before it was too late.

"Thank you, Chief," I whispered, my voice choked with emotion. "I don't know what I would do without your guidance."

He smiled, his eyes filled with warmth and understanding. "We're all in this together, Keisha. You're not alone in this fight."

With renewed determination, I left Chief Donovan's office, ready to face the challenges ahead. I knew that the road to recovery would not be easy, and that there would be setbacks along the way. But I also knew that I had the support of my colleagues, my friends, and my family – and that together, we would conquer the flames that threatened to consume us all.

Over the following weeks, I threw myself into the task of healing, both physically and mentally. I began setting boundaries around my work, forcing myself to step away from the computer and the notepad when my allocated hours were up. At first, it was difficult to switch off, but gradually, I found myself able to relax and enjoy my time away from the job.

I started to pay more attention to my diet, filling my meals with fresh fruits, vegetables, and lean proteins. I began a regular exercise routine, going for daily jogs along the beach, and taking up yoga to help clear my mind and relieve stress. And most importantly, I made a concerted effort to sleep more, ensuring that I got a full eight hours of rest each night.

As I began to feel stronger and more centered, I reached out to the friends and family that I had neglected. I apologized for my absence and made a promise to be more present in their lives. To my relief, they welcomed me back with open arms, offering their love and support as I continued my journey towards recovery.

Slowly but surely, I felt the fog of burnout begin to lift. My energy levels increased, my mood improved, and my passion for my work reignited. And as I returned to the front lines of the battle against the arsonists, I found myself better equipped to handle the stress and challenges that came my way.

Armed with a newfound sense of balance and resilience, I knew that I could face whatever the future held. For I was Keisha Harper – journalist, fire chaser, and survivor – and I would not be defeated.

The Arrest of the Arsonist

T he sultry Miami sun was a relentless force, bearing down on the city like a fiery hammer. The air was thick with humidity, making each breath feel like a battle for survival. But despite the oppressive heat, a sense of anticipation hung in the air, electric and palpable. Word had spread throughout the Miami Sentinel newsroom that the police were closing in on the arsonist who had tormented the city for months, leaving a trail of smoldering ruins in their wake. And I, Keisha Harper, was determined to be there when the story reached its dramatic climax.

The past few weeks had been a whirlwind of activity, with leads and tips pouring in from every corner of the city. My colleagues and I had chased down every scrap of information, following the arsonist's trail like bloodhounds on the hunt. And now, finally, it seemed as though our persistence was about to pay off.

As I stood outside the newsroom, waiting for my ride to the scene, I couldn't help but feel a mixture of excitement and apprehension. The arrest of the arsonist would mark the end of a long and grueling chapter in my life – but it would also bring closure to the countless victims whose lives had been irrevocably altered by the fires. And as I thought about the pain and suffering that had been left in the arsonist's wake, I knew that I had to be there to witness the moment when justice was finally served.

As the unmarked police car pulled up to the curb, I felt a sudden surge of adrenaline coursing through my veins. This was it – the culmination of months of tireless investigation and dogged determination. And as I slid into the back seat, my heart pounding in my chest, I vowed to myself that I would see this story through to the very end.

We sped through the city, weaving through traffic with the grace and precision of a predatory animal on the hunt. My pulse quickened with each passing mile, the anticipation building within me like a tidal wave. But as we neared our destination, I couldn't shake the feeling that there was still one final piece of the puzzle that had yet to fall into place.

We arrived at the scene, a nondescript warehouse in an industrial part of town. The area was swarming with police officers and firefighters, their faces etched with determination and focus. I could see the fire chief, Donovan, standing near the entrance, barking orders to his team as they prepared to breach the building.

I approached him, my notebook clutched tightly in my hand. "Chief Donovan," I called out, my voice barely audible above the din of the emergency vehicles. "What's the situation?"

He turned to face me, his eyes alight with a fierce intensity. "We've got the bastard cornered, Keisha," he replied, his voice tight with emotion. "This ends tonight."

A shiver ran down my spine at his words, and I knew that I was standing on the precipice of history. The fate of the city – and the lives of countless innocent people – hung in the balance, and I was there to bear witness.

As the SWAT team prepared to enter the warehouse, I took up my position behind a nearby squad car, my eyes fixed on the building's entrance. I could feel the tension in the air, thick and palpable, as the officers readied themselves for the confrontation that was about to unfold. And as the team leader gave the signal to move in, I held my breath, praying that they would succeed in their mission to apprehend the arsonist.

The sound of breaking glass and splintering wood filled the air as the SWAT team stormed the building, their movements swift and precise. I strained my ears, trying to pick up any sounds that might indicate the progress of the raid. The seconds stretched out like hours, each passing moment an eternity of suspense and anticipation.

Suddenly, I heard the faint crackle of a police radio, and my heart leapt into my throat. The voice on the other end was tense but triumphant, and I knew that they had succeeded in capturing the arsonist. As the officers began to emerge from the warehouse, I caught my first glimpse of the man responsible for so much pain and destruction.

He was a wiry figure, his face gaunt and hollow from months of living in the shadows. His eyes darted nervously about, taking in the sea of armed officers that surrounded him, and I could see the fear and desperation in their depths. But as he was led past me, our eyes met for the briefest of moments – and in that instant, I saw the cold, unrepentant spark of a man who had no remorse for his actions.

As the arsonist was loaded into the back of a waiting police car, I felt a strange mixture of relief and sadness. The specter of fear and destruction that had haunted the city for so long was finally vanquished – but the scars left by his actions would remain for years to come.

As the excitement of the arrest began to fade, I realized that I had a job to do. I interviewed the officers involved in the raid, piecing together the dramatic story of the arsonist's capture. I spoke with the victims of his fires, their faces etched with a mixture of relief and lingering pain. And as I put pen to paper, weaving their stories into a narrative that would captivate our readers, I felt a sense of pride and accomplishment that I had not experienced in months.

As the sun began to set on the city, casting long shadows across the skyline, I knew that my work was done. The arsonist had been brought to justice, and the city could begin the long and arduous process of healing. But as I reflected on the events of the day, I realized that there was one more task that I needed to complete – one more story that I needed to tell.

I made my way back to the Miami Sentinel newsroom, the weight of my notebook heavy in my hands. I knew that I had a responsibility to share the story of the arsonist's capture with the world – but I also knew that I had a responsibility to myself.

As I sat down at my desk, my fingers hovering over the keyboard, I made a decision. I would write the story of the arsonist's capture, of the brave men and women who had brought him to justice, and of the city that had endured so much pain and loss. But once the story was written, once the ink had dried and the presses had rolled, I would take a step back. I would take the time that I needed to heal, to recover from the burnout that had plagued me for so long.

I knew that it would not be an easy journey, that there would be days when the temptation to return to my old habits would be almost overwhelming. But I also knew that I owed it to myself, and to the people who cared about me, to find a way to balance my passion for journalism with my need for self-care and rest.

So, as I began to type the first words of the story that would define my career, I made a silent promise to myself. I would write the story, and I would write it well – but I would also take the time to heal, to find the balance that I had been seeking for so long. And as I watched the words appear on the screen before me, I knew that I had taken the first step on the path to a brighter, healthier future. A future where I could continue to chase the truth and bring justice to light, but also one where I could nurture my own well-being and happiness. As the final sentences flowed from my fingertips, I felt a sense of accomplishment and serenity wash over me. The chapter of the arsonist was closed, and a new chapter of growth, healing, and self-discovery was just beginning.

Keisha's Sabbatical Plans

Keisha

I sit in front of my laptop, staring at the screen, feeling the weight of exhaustion pressing down on my shoulders. The past year has been a relentless pursuit of truth, chasing leads, and investigating the string of arson cases that plagued Miami. I've poured my heart and soul into this job, but now I'm burnt out, my passion flickering like a dying flame. I need a break, a chance to escape the suffocating routine and recharge my spirit.

I spend hours researching and thinking about where I want to go. After much contemplation, I make a decision that both scares and excites me—I'm going to take a two-month sabbatical in Montego Bay, Jamaica. I've never been there before, but the allure of its vibrant culture, breathtaking landscapes, and serene beaches call to me like a siren's song.

I spend another three hours looking for the best place to stay and the hidden gems to explore in Montego Bay. I want this sabbatical to be a transformative experience, an opportunity to immerse myself in a new environment and embrace the beauty of the island. I come across pictures of pristine beaches, vibrant coral reefs, and lush rain forests that make my heart skip a beat. It's a paradise waiting to be discovered, and I can't wait to lose myself in its wonders.

Finally, I settle on a cozy beachfront villa tucked away in a secluded corner of Montego Bay. It offers privacy and tranquility, the perfect setting for introspection and reflection. I envision myself waking up to the sound of gentle waves crashing against the shore, feeling the warm embrace of the sun on my skin as I sip a cup of local Jamaican coffee.

As I book my flights and accommodation, a mix of nervousness and anticipation courses through my veins. It's a leap into the unknown, a chance to rediscover myself and find solace away from the chaos of my everyday life. Montego Bay promises a sanctuary where I can rejuvenate my weary soul.

I call my boss at the Sentinel and tell her that I am taking a sabbatical. After everything that has happened recently, I am burnt out and need a break. I tell her that I have booked my trip and will be leaving in four weeks. That gives us time to find someone to ghostwrite my column before I leave and me time to get them acclimated to my writing style.

****

Looking for a ghostwriter to fill in while I am on sabbatical is adding more stress to my burnout. I will be so happy when I can get on that plane. I have never felt like this before. I really need to decompress.

As my sabbatical in Montego Bay progresses, a sense of tranquility settles within me. The sun-kissed beaches and vibrant culture have woven their magic, rejuvenating my

16

spirit and allowing me to find solace in the present moment. However, there's a nagging thought in the back of my mind—a responsibility that still lingers despite my distance from the Miami Sentinel. My column.

With a heavy heart, I realize that I cannot fully detach from my role as a journalist. The Miami Sentinel relies on my weekly insights, and leaving a void in my absence is not an option. Determined to find a solution, I reach out to my boss, Mr. Thompson, and propose the idea of bringing in a ghostwriter to pen my column while I'm on sabbatical.

To my surprise, Mr. Thompson agrees, seeing it as an opportunity to explore new perspectives and maintain the continuity of the column. We embark on the search for the perfect ghostwriter—a talented individual who can seamlessly step into my shoes and capture the essence of my writing style.

Together, Mr. Thompson and I schedule a series of interviews with potential candidates. The first applicant is a seasoned journalist named Rebecca Simmons, known for her thought-provoking pieces on social justice issues. We sit in Mr. Thompson's office, anxiously waiting for Rebecca to arrive.

When Rebecca walks through the door, there's an air of confidence about her. She exudes a quiet intelligence and carries herself with a poised grace. As we engage in conversation, I can't help but admire her eloquence and the way her eyes light up when discussing the power of storytelling.

Rebecca shares her vision for the column, emphasizing the importance of staying true to its core values while infusing her own unique perspectives. She understands the delicate balance between honoring the established readership and bringing fresh insights to the table. It's clear that she has done her research and possesses a genuine passion for journalism.

As the interview progresses, I find myself increasingly convinced that Rebecca might just be the perfect fit. Her ideas align with my own, and I can envision her seamlessly stepping into my role, breathing new life into the column. A sense of relief washes over me, knowing that my absence will not leave a void but instead open doors for exciting new possibilities.

I glance at Mr. Thompson, and there's a twinkle in his eyes—a silent agreement that Rebecca is indeed a strong contender. He leans back in his chair, contemplating our conversation.

"Rebecca, we appreciate your enthusiasm and your evident commitment to journalistic integrity," Mr. Thompson begins. "If you were to step into Keisha's role, what would your responsibilities entail?"

Rebecca leans forward, her voice steady and confident. "First and foremost, I would honor the spirit of Keisha's column, ensuring that its essence remains intact. I would diligently research and present compelling topics that align with the readership's interests. With Keisha's guidance, I would strive to capture her unique voice while infusing my own perspectives to provide a fresh take on current issues.

I nod in agreement, impressed by Rebecca's understanding of the delicate balance required for this undertaking. It's reassuring to know that she recognizes the importance of maintaining the connection with our readers while bringing her own touch to the column.

Mr. Thompson leans forward, his gaze shifting between us. "Keisha, what are your thoughts on Rebecca taking over your column during your sabbatical?"

A mixture of emotions swirl within me. There's a twinge of reluctance, an attachment to something I've poured my heart and soul into for so long. But beneath that hesitation, there's also a sense of excitement—an opportunity for growth, for someone else to share their unique perspectives with our readers. I take a deep breath, steadying myself before responding.

"Mr. Thompson, I believe Rebecca has the skills and passion necessary to uphold the integrity of my column while infusing it with her own voice. I trust her ability to engage our readers and deliver thought-provoking content. While it's not easy for me to step back, I understand the importance of allowing the column to evolve and embrace new perspectives. I believe Rebecca is the right person to take on this responsibility."

A smile spreads across Mr. Thompson's face, a sign of his approval. "Excellent. It seems we're all in agreement then. Rebecca, welcome to the team."

Rebecca's face lights up with a mixture of gratitude and excitement. "Thank you both. I'm honored to have this opportunity and I look forward to working closely with Keisha to ensure a smooth transition."

With the decision made, we dive into the specifics of the arrangement. We discuss deadlines, communication channels, and the collaborative nature of our partnership. It's important for me to stay involved in the process, to provide guidance and share my insights while allowing Rebecca the freedom to explore her own ideas.

As our conversation unfolds, a sense of relief washes over me. I realize that by entrusting my column to a talented and passionate writer like Rebecca, I can truly embrace my sabbatical and the journey of self-discovery it offers. The weight of responsibility begins to lift, replaced by a newfound sense of liberation.

Leaving Mr. Thompson's office, I feel a sense of anticipation for the next chapter of my sabbatical. I know that while I may be physically distant from the Miami Sentinel, a part of me will still be there, carried forward by the words and insights of Rebecca and the continuation of the column.

As I walk along the sun-drenched shores of Montego Bay, a gentle breeze caressing my skin, I can't help but feel grateful for the unexpected twists and turns that life brings. Change can be daunting, but it also carries the potential for growth and transformation. And in this moment, I embrace the unknown, eager to witness the evolution of my column and the journeys it will take readers on under Rebecca's capable pen.

Llanzo Trying to Move On

Llanzo

I stand at the helm of my boat, the warm Caribbean breeze caressing my face as I guide the vessel through the crystal-clear waters. The vibrant hues of turquoise and emerald surround me, a kaleidoscope of colors that only serves as a stark contrast to the darkness that resides within my heart. It has been two years since my beloved wife passed away, and not a day goes by without feeling the deep ache of her absence.

Losing her was like losing a part of myself, a void that cannot be filled no matter how hard I try. Her laughter, her touch, her unwavering support—I cherish every memory, holding them close to my soul like fragile treasures. But the pain of her loss still lingers, a constant reminder of the fragility of life and the harsh realities that we all must face.

In the wake of her passing, I buried myself in my work, dedicating my time and energy to the excursion company we built together. The turquoise waters that once brought us joy and serenity now serve as a constant reminder of the dreams we had shared, the adventures we had embarked upon. I find solace in the routine, the daily tasks that keep me occupied and distract my mind from the painful memories.

Owning the excursion company has become my refuge, a way to fill the void and find a semblance of purpose in this new chapter of my life. I pour myself into every aspect of the business, ensuring that every excursion is meticulously planned, every guest's experience unforgettable. The smiles on their faces and the joy in their voices momentarily lift the weight from my shoulders, allowing me to find moments of respite amidst the tumultuous sea of grief.

But beneath the surface, a part of me is still adrift, lost in the currents of sorrow and longing. I cannot fathom the idea of falling in love again, of opening my heart to the possibility of losing another cherished soul. The pain of my wife's absence has etched its mark on me, leaving scars that I fear will never fade. Love, once a beacon of light in my life, now carries the weight of past sorrows, an elusive and treacherous path that I dare not tread.

As I navigate the shimmering waters, memories of our adventures together flood my mind. The sunsets we witnessed, hand in hand, painting the sky in breathtaking hues of orange and gold. The moonlit walks along the shore, where we whispered dreams and aspirations to the stars above. It is in these moments that the ache intensifies, the longing for her touch overwhelming.

Yet, amidst the melancholy, I find glimpses of hope, fragile rays of light that seep through the cracks in my wounded heart. The laughter of a child on one of our family-friendly excursions, the warmth of a genuine connection forged with a fellow adventurer. These moments remind me that life still holds the potential for joy, that there are treasures yet to be discovered amidst the waves of grief.

I know that my journey toward healing will be long and arduous, filled with ups and downs, but I am determined to navigate these treacherous waters with resilience and grace. I will honor my wife's memory by embracing the beauty of life, even in the face of heartache. And perhaps, in time, I will find the courage to allow love to find its way back into my heart, to let another soul touch the depths of my being and bring solace to the loneliness that haunts me.

But for now, as I guide my boat through the azure waters, I find solace in the rhythm of the sea, in the embrace of the gentle waves. My journey toward healing has only just begun, and I am prepared to weather the storms that lie ahead, knowing that with each passing day I grow stronger, slowly mending the fragments of my shattered heart. Life without my wife will never be the same, and I have accepted that. But as I continue to bury myself in my work, I find solace in the moments of connection with others, in the bonds forged through shared experiences and the laughter that fills the air. The excursion company has become not only a business but also a vessel for healing, a conduit through which I can channel my love and passion.

The turquoise waters that surround me now carry a bittersweet beauty. They mirror the complexity of my emotions—calm and serene on the surface, but hiding depths of sorrow and longing below. In the midst of nature's splendor, I seek solace and find fragments of peace. The rhythm of the waves, the caress of the salty breeze, they remind me that life continues to flow, even in the face of heartache.

As I navigate through each day since she passed, I carry my wife's memory with me, woven into the fabric of my being. Her spirit whispers in the wind, guiding me forward with a gentle touch. I find solace in knowing that she would want me to embrace the beauty of life, to find happiness in the small moments that grace my path.

And so, I continue to explore the turquoise depths, to share the wonders of the ocean with those who seek adventure and respite. The excursion company thrives, not just as a business venture but as a testament to the resilience of the human spirit. Through the joy and laughter of our guests, I find fleeting moments of contentment, reminders that life's tapestry is interwoven with both joy and sorrow.

While I cannot predict the future or the winding paths it may lead me down, I am open to the possibility of love finding its way back into my life. The wounds of loss will forever leave their mark, but they do not define me. I choose to honor my wife's memory by living fully, by cherishing the beauty of every sunrise and sunset, and by sharing the beauty of the world with those who cross my path.

I close my eyes, and the memory washes over me like the gentle waves lapping against the hull of our boat. It's a memory of Mara—my beloved wife—and our unforgettable adventure out on the crystal-clear waters of Montego Bay.

I can feel the warmth of the sun on my skin as Mara and I board our boat, excitement bubbling within us. The vibrant hues of the Caribbean Sea stretch out before us, a breathtaking mosaic of blues and greens. Our laughter dances through the air as we exchange playful banter, our love for each other evident in every word and smile.

As we sail towards the reef, anticipation builds within me. Mara's eyes sparkle with delight, mirroring my own. We anchor near a thriving coral garden, and our snorkeling gear is secured. With each dive into the cool water, a world of wonder unfolds beneath us.

The underwater realm welcomes us with open arms. Schools of neon-colored fish dart by, their scales shimmering like living rainbows. Mara's laughter bubbles through her snorkel as she points to a majestic parrotfish, its vibrant hues blending seamlessly with the surrounding coral.

We glide through the water hand in hand, our fingers intertwined, as if to ensure we never drift apart. A sense of serenity envelopes us as we become one with the underwater paradise. The rhythmic swaying of the coral fans and the gentle sway of the fish create a symphony of tranquility.

A sudden surge of excitement fills the water around us as a group of playful nurse sharks emerges from the depths. Their sleek bodies move with grace and power, captivating our attention. Mara's eyes widen with awe, and I can't help but smile at her infectious enthusiasm.

We watch as the sharks gracefully navigate the reef, their presence commanding respect and admiration. They glide effortlessly, their silhouettes casting shadows on the sandy ocean floor. Mara's voice echoes through the water as she marvels at their beauty, her words carried by the currents.

"Can you believe this, Llanzo?" she exclaims, her voice muffled by her snorkel. "It's like we've stepped into a whole new world. The colors, the fish, the sharks—it's magical."

I squeeze her hand, my heart overflowing with love. "It truly is, Mara. And experiencing it with you makes it all the more extraordinary."

We spend what feels like an eternity exploring the reef, our souls intertwining with the enchanting marine life. Time loses its meaning as we revel in the beauty of this underwater sanctuary, a sanctuary we are fortunate enough to call our own, even if just for a fleeting moment.

Eventually, we resurface, gasping for air but filled with a sense of contentment. The boat awaits us, bobbing gently on the surface, ready to carry us back to the shores of reality. But the memory of that reef snorkeling adventure will forever remain etched in my heart—a testament to the love we shared, the joy we experienced, and the boundless beauty that surrounded us.

Mara's laughter still echoes in my ears, her smile imprinted in my mind. Though she is no longer physically with me, I carry her spirit within me, a guiding light that illuminates my path. And every time I find myself near the water, I can't help but think of that magical day—the day we ventured into the depths of the sea, hand in hand, and discovered a world beyond our wildest dreams.

As the sun begins to set on another day in Montego Bay, I find solace in the quietude of the horizon. The hues of pink and orange paint the sky, casting a soft glow on the waters below. In this moment, I embrace the fragile balance between grief and resilience, between honoring the past and embracing the present.

Life without my wife will always carry a sense of loss, but I am determined to forge a path toward healing, to find moments of joy amidst the echoes of sorrow. And as I guide my boat back to the shore, I do so with a renewed sense of purpose, knowing that the excursion company not only allows me to share the wonders of the sea but also serves as a vessel for my own healing.

Arrival in Montego Bay

Keisha

The day of departure arrives, and I find myself standing in the bustling Miami International Airport, a sense of freedom mingling with the hum of excitement around me. Clutching my passport and boarding pass, I take a deep breath, ready to embark on this new adventure. The airplane engines roar to life, propelling me into the unknown, and I can't help but feel a surge of anticipation bubble within me.

As the plane touches down at 8 o'clock that morning in Montego Bay, Jamaica, I navigate my way through the airport, I emerge into a vibrant sea of people, their laughter and chatter creating a symphony of sound. The Jamaican rhythm pulses through the air, the infectious beat beckoning me to join in the celebration of life. I hail a taxi, the driver's friendly smile and laid-back demeanor instantly putting me at ease.

As we drive through the streets of Montego Bay, I'm capti-vated by the eclectic mix of architecture, a blend of colonial charm and colorful Caribbean flair. The bustling marketplaces, with their vibrant stalls and the melodic cadence of vendors calling out their wares, offer a glimpse into the heart and soul of this captivating city.

Arriving at my hotel, I'm greeted by a warm and inviting atmosphere. The receptionist, with her welcoming smile, presents me with a keycard, and I make my way to my room. Unlocking the door, I'm met with a breathtaking view of the sparkling turquoise waters stretching out before me—a sight that instantly soothes my weary soul.

The the tropical heat envelops me like a warm embrace. Stepping onto the tarmac, I'm greeted by a kaleidoscope of colors—a vivid tapestry of lush greenery, azure skies, and vibrant flowers in bloom. The air is alive with the intoxicating scents of exotic spices and ocean breezes, instantly putting me at ease.

I am excited to start exploring and decide to head out into town. I immerse myself in the rhythm of Montego Bay. I wander through the narrow, colorful streets, getting lost in the maze of vibrant shops and quaint cafes. The tantalizing aromas of jerk chicken and fresh fruits waft through the air, tempting me to indulge in the local culinary delights.

Eager to delve deeper into Jamaican culture, I embark on a journey of exploration and discovery. I join a guided tour to the famous Dunn's River Falls, where I navigate the cascading waters, feeling a surge of exhilaration as I conquer each step. The natural beauty envelops me, the misty spray refreshing my senses and rejuvenating my spirit.

The sun kisses my skin as I relax on the powdery white sand of the renowned Doctor's Cave Beach. The crystal-clear waters beckon me, and I wade in, feeling the gentle caress of the waves against my legs. Floating on my back, I gaze up at the endless expanse of the sky, the worries of the world slipping away with each passing cloud.

That evening, I find myself drawn to the vibrant nightlife that Montego Bay has to offer. The pulsating reggae beats fill the air as I dance the night away with locals and fellow travelers alike. The infectious laughter and carefree spirit of the Jamaican people uplift my own, reminding me of the joy that life has to offer.

****

As day two unfolds, I gradually shed the weight of my responsibilities, allowing myself to fully embrace the present moment. I find solace in the simple pleasures—a lazy afternoon spent in a hammock, swaying gently beneath the shade of palm trees, the pages of a captivating novel turning in my hands.

Amidst the enchantment of Montego Bay, I can't help but notice a transformation within myself. The heaviness that burdened my heart begins to dissipate, replaced by a newfound lightness and a renewed sense of purpose. The vibrant energy of the city seeps into my being, igniting a spark within me that had been dimmed for far too long.

Yet, amidst the serenity, there is a lingering longing within me—a desire for connection, for a deeper human experience. It's a feeling I can't shake, an ache that resonates deep within my soul. Little do I know that the universe has something extraordinary in store for me, something that will awaken my heart in ways I never imagined.

As the warm Jamaican sun bathes my skin, a sense of liberation begins to seep into my bones. Montego Bay has worked its magic on me, slowly peeling away the layers of stress and exhaustion that had consumed me back in Miami. In this tropical paradise, I find myself letting go, allowing the worries of my demanding job to fade into the distance.

I lounge on a comfortable beach chair, the soft sand caressing my toes. The rhythmic sound of crashing waves creates a soothing backdrop, lulling me into a state of tranquility. Closing my eyes, I inhale the salty breeze, feeling a weight lift off my shoulders. It's a moment of pure bliss—a moment I've longed for, but never truly allowed myself to experience.

As I open my eyes, I notice the vibrant colors surrounding me—the azure sky stretching endlessly overhead, the emerald palm trees swaying gracefully in the gentle breeze. Nature's palette is alive and vivid, a stark contrast to the muted hues of my hectic city life. It's as if the world is painting a vivid portrait, inviting me to immerse myself in its beauty.

With a newfound sense of freedom coursing through my veins, I decide to embrace the spontaneity that Montego Bay offers. I slip off my sandals, feeling the warmth of the sand between my toes, and head towards the water's edge. The crystal-clear turquoise waves beckon me, their playful whispers coaxing me to let go of inhibitions and dive into the unknown.

A mischievous grin spreads across my face as I wade into the inviting water. The coolness washes over me, refreshing my body and soul. I feel a surge of exhilaration as I surrender to the gentle currents, allowing them to guide me further into the embrace of the sea.

As I swim, I relish in the freedom of movement, reveling in the weightlessness that only the ocean can provide. The cares and concerns that once burdened my mind are carried away by the waves, replaced with a newfound sense of lightness and joy.

I dive beneath the surface, immersing myself in an underwater wonderland. The vibrant coral reefs come to life, teeming with an array of fish, their kaleidoscopic scales reflecting the sunlight. I am mesmerized by their graceful dance, their synchronized movements captivating my attention. In this moment, I become a part of their world, a silent observer in a symphony of aquatic life.

As I resurface, my laughter mingles with the sound of crashing waves. It's a sound I haven't heard in far too long—a sound that reminds me of the simple pleasures of life, the ones I had forgotten amidst the chaos of my career. Montego Bay has become my catalyst for rediscovery, reminding me of the importance of embracing the present moment and allowing myself to let loose.

I swim back to shore, my body glowing with a newfound energy. As I settle back into my beach chair, I can't help but feel a renewed sense of purpose. The weight of responsibility no longer hangs heavily over me; instead, I embrace the notion of balance—the delicate harmony between work and play, ambition and relaxation.

With each passing moment in Montego Bay, I feel the layers of stress peeling away, revealing the vibrant, adventurous spirit that has long been dormant within me. I am no longer confined by the boundaries I've created for myself. I am free to explore, to indulge, to find joy in the simplest of pleasures.

As the sun sets on another idyllic day in Montego Bay, I find myself sitting at a beach side café, sipping on a refreshing cocktail. The soft glow of the fading sunlight casts a golden hue over the surroundings, creating an ethereal atmosphere. And in this moment, as if guided by fate itself, our paths are destined to cross—the meeting of two souls amidst the backdrop of paradise.

Meeting Llanzo

Keisha

Day Three

As the sun rises over Montego Bay, casting a golden glow on the azure waters, I wake up with a renewed sense of excitement. Today, I have booked an excursion to go snorkeling with reef sharks—an adventure that promises both thrills and the opportunity to immerse myself in the mesmerizing beauty of the underwater world. Little do I know that this day will mark the beginning of a chapter I never expected to write.

I make my way to the designated meeting point, a small dock where the excursion boats are docked. The air is filled with the scent of saltwater and anticipation. I'm surrounded by a group of fellow adventure seekers, their eyes shimmering with a mix of excitement and nervousness. We exchange small talk, sharing snippets of our lives and the reasons that brought us to Montego Bay.

As the boat sets sail, I find myself drawn to the breathtaking panorama unfolding before my eyes. The cerulean sea stretches out endlessly, the rhythmic swells of the waves hypnotic in their dance. I take a deep breath, inhaling the fresh ocean breeze that carries the promise of an unforgettable experience.

The boat anchors near a vibrant coral reef, teeming with a kaleidoscope of colorful marine life. The moment has arrived—I slip into the cool embrace of the water, donning my snorkeling gear, and let myself be immersed in a world beyond imagination. The water envelopes me, and I swim among schools of tropical fish, their iridescent scales glistening in the sunlight.

I slip on my snorkeling gear, feeling a mix of excitement and anticipation. Today is the day I dive into the mesmerizing world beneath the surface, exploring the vibrant reef that lies beneath the sparkling waters of Montego Bay. As I step off the boat and into the cool embrace of the ocean, my senses come alive, and I'm immediately immersed in a kaleidoscope of colors and sounds.

As I lower my face into the water, a whole new realm reveals itself before my eyes. The coral formations, like intricate sculptures, rise from the sandy seabed, their vibrant hues creating a breathtaking underwater city. Each coral branch houses a delicate ecosystem, teeming with life. It's as if I've stumbled upon a hidden paradise, a world pulsating with energy and beauty.

I swim along the edge of a massive brain coral, marveling at its intricate patterns and the rainbow of fish darting in and out of its crevices. Schools of vibrant tropical fish glide by, their scales shimmering in the sunlight. Electric blue tangs, dazzling yellow angelfish, and playful clownfish with their distinctive stripes—all coexist in perfect harmony, creating a mesmerizing underwater ballet.

As I venture deeper, I encounter an enchanting garden of soft corals. They sway gracefully with the ebb and flow of the current, their tendrils resembling delicate ribbons in the water. The mesmerizing colors of pink, purple, and orange paint the scene, casting an ethereal glow that is simply captivating. It's like swimming through a living dreamscape, where reality and fantasy intertwine.

I come across a group of graceful sea turtles, their majestic presence commanding respect. With a few effortless strokes of their flippers, they glide effortlessly through the water, embodying a sense of tranquility that washes over me. Their ancient wisdom seems to emanate from their wise eyes, as if they hold the secrets of the ocean within them.

A gentle movement catches my eye, and I turn to witness the spectacle of a spotted eagle ray gracefully soaring through the water. Its wings undulate with elegance, propelling it forward in a seemingly weightless dance. It's a fleeting encounter, but one that etches itself into my memory, a reminder of the awe-inspiring wonders that lie beneath the surface.

I venture closer to a rocky outcrop, where a bustling community of vibrant marine life awaits. I spot a camouflaged octopus, its mesmerizing ability to blend into its surroundings leaving me in awe. A curious moray eel peers out from its hidden crevice, its piercing eyes fixed upon me. It's a thrilling moment of connection, as if I am being welcomed into their world, even if just for a fleeting moment.

The gentle presence of nurse sharks catches my attention, their sleek forms gliding gracefully across the sandy bottom. Fear and fascination intertwine within me, and I watch as the sharks glide effortlessly, their presence commanding respect. They exude a serene calmness, defying the misconceptions often associated with their species. It's a humbling experience to witness these powerful creatures in their natural habitat, a reminder of the importance of respecting and protecting our marine environments.

As I reluctantly resurface, the warm sun kisses my face, and I can't help but feel a profound sense of gratitude. The underwater journey I've embarked upon has left an indelible mark on my soul. It's a reminder of the vastness and beauty of the natural world, and of my own place within it. Montego Bay's reef has unveiled a world beyond imagination—a world that invites exploration, inspires wonder, and connects us to something greater than ourselves.

Lost in this surreal experience, I barely notice the approaching figure. But when our eyes meet, time seems to stand still. Llanzo Wright, the owner of the excursion company, stands before me, his eyes twinkling with a mixture of warmth and mischief. His sun-kissed skin and effortless charm leave me momentarily breathless.

"Are you enjoying the show?" he asks, his voice carrying the melodic lilt of Jamaica. His smile is infectious, and I find myself returning it, a flutter of anticipation stirring within me.

"Yes, it's incredible," I reply, my voice tinged with wonder.

Llanzo's gaze lingers on me, as if he can see beyond the surface—an understanding passing between us, unspoken but palpable. There's an undeniable chemistry, an electric current that crackles in the air, and it both thrills and unnerves me.

We swim side by side, the reef sharks gracefully circling us as if we're part of their watery realm. Llanzo shares his wealth of knowledge about the marine life, pointing out hidden wonders and guiding me through this underwater paradise. His passion for the ocean is contagious, and I find myself captivated not only by the vibrant ecosystem but also by the depth of his spirit.

After resurfacing, and as we swim back towards the boat, I carry with me a renewed appreciation for the delicate balance of life beneath the waves, and an unwavering desire to protect and preserve it for generations to come. We find ourselves seated on the boat, our bodies still buzzing with the thrill of the encounter. Llanzo's eyes meet mine, and in that moment, it's as if the world fades away, leaving only the two of us.

"You have an adventurous spirit," he says, his voice tinged with admiration. "Not many are brave enough to swim with sharks."

I laugh softly, a mix of exhilaration and vulnerability coursing through me. "I guess I needed a break from routine, a chance to feel truly alive."

Llanzo nods, his gaze intense yet tender. "Sometimes, it takes stepping out of our comfort zones to discover the depths of our own resilience and passion."

As the boat sails back towards the shore, a bittersweet feeling settles within me. The instant connection I feel with Llanzo tugs at my heart, but the walls I've built to protect myself urge caution. I remind myself of my initial decision—to not get involved with anyone during my sabbatical. Yet, in Llanzo's presence, that resolve wavers like a flickering flame.

We part ways at the dock, promising to meet again for another adventure. His parting words linger in the air, echoing in my mind long after he disappears from view. The spark ignited between us, though unspoken, feels undeniable—a force too strong to ignore.

As I return to my hotel room, I find myself torn between

the familiar safety of my solitude and the magnetic pull of the connection I've found in Llanzo. Thoughts swirl in my mind, a tempest of conflicting desires. Can I allow myself to take a chance on love? Can I open my heart to the possibility of a profound connection, even if it defies my self-imposed boundaries?

Night falls over Montego Bay, casting a cloak of darkness that mirrors the uncertainty within me. I stand at the balcony, gazing at the moonlit ocean, its gentle waves whispering secrets of the universe. In this moment of contemplation, I realize that sometimes the most extraordinary chapters of our lives are born from unexpected encounters, from the willingness to embrace the unknown.

With a mix of trepidation and curiosity, I make a silent vow to myself—to follow the path that unfolds before me, to allow the rhythm of Montego Bay to guide me towards a truth that transcends fear. For in the depths of my soul, I sense that this connection with Llanzo holds the potential to heal the burnout that has plagued my spirit, to ignite a fire within me that burns brighter than ever before.

And so, as the night embraces the world, I drift into sleep, knowing that the dawn of a new day will bring with it the promise of exploration, of discovery, and the continuation of a story that has only just begun.

Llanzo's Past

Llanzo

The sun hangs low in the sky as I spot Keisha sitting on the beach, her presence like a beacon in the fading daylight. Something inside me compels me to join her, to share a moment of vulnerability amidst the tranquility of this Jamaican paradise. I walk towards her, feeling a mix of nervousness and anticipation, unsure of how to navigate the complexities of my past.

As I approach, Keisha looks up, her eyes filled with curiosity and warmth. She smiles, and it's as if a weight lifts off my shoulders, emboldening me to open up about the pain that has shaped my present. We exchange a few words, and then we start walking along the shore, the rhythmic sound of the waves providing a comforting backdrop to our conversation.

With each step, my heart pounds, echoing the memories I'm about to unearth. I take a deep breath, trying to steady my voice as I begin to share the story that has haunted me for the past two years. The weight of the words rests heavy on my tongue, but I know it's time to release them, to let Keisha into the depths of my past.

"I lost my wife, Mara, in a car accident," I begin, my voice a mere whisper against the crashing waves. "It happened two years ago, but the pain still lingers, as fresh as if it were yesterday."

Keisha's gaze remains fixed on me, her eyes filled with empathy and understanding. I find solace in her presence, knowing that she is willing to listen, to hold the fragments of my broken heart as I piece them together.

"Mara, my beloved wife, was a vision of grace and beauty that words struggle to capture. She possessed an enchanting allure that left an indelible mark on anyone fortunate enough to lay eyes upon her. Her presence alone brightened a room, drawing people in with her warm smile and magnetic personality. Her eyes, oh, her eyes. They are the color of the Caribbean sea on a clear summer day—deep and mesmerizing, twinkling with a hint of mischief. They reflect a depth of emotion that transcends mere words, speaking volumes without uttering a sound. In those eyes, I found solace, love, and a glimpse into her soul. Her hair, was cascading in waves of ebony silk, that framed her face delicately. Each strand seemed to carry a lustrous shine, reflecting the sun's rays as if it were woven with strands of stardust. I recall the countless moments spent running my fingers through that silky mane, feeling the softness beneath my touch, and reveling in the intimacy it fostered. Her smile, radiant and infectious, has the power to brighten even the darkest of days. It dances upon her lips, unveiling a glimpse of her inner joy and illuminating the world around her. How I miss that smile, its ability to chase away my worries and melt

40

my heart with its sheer radiance. Mara's laughter, like a melody floating on the wind, is a symphony of pure happiness. It fills the air, echoing through our shared memories, and lifts my spirits in its gentle embrace. I can still hear the sound, so full of life and love, resonating in my mind, a cherished treasure that I hold dear. Her touch, oh, her touch. It lingers upon my skin like the gentle caress of a summer breeze, igniting a spark within me that ignites my senses. Whether it's the brush of her hand against mine or the warmth of her embrace, every touch conveys a tenderness and affection that words struggle to convey. It is a language of love that only we share. And her presence, her mere presence, fills the room with an undeniable energy. When Mara enters a space, it comes alive with a vibrant aura that envelops everyone around her. She radiates a warmth and authenticity that draws people in, captivating their hearts and leaving a lasting impression. But beyond her physical attributes, it is Mara's spirit that truly captivates me. She embodies strength, resilience, and an unwavering love that transcends time and space. Her unwavering support, her unwavering belief in me, has been a guiding light in my darkest hours. Each memory of Mara is etched deeply within my heart, a testament to the love we shared. Though she may be physically absent, her essence remains an integral part of my being. Her beauty, both outward and inward, continues to inspire me, to guide me, and to remind me of the immense love we once shared. And so, as I recount these details of Mara's physical appearance, I am reminded of the depth of emotions she evokes within me. She is not simply a collection of features but a manifestation of love, a beacon of light that forever illuminates my path. Her beauty, both external and internal, is a reflection of the love we shared, a love that will forever live on in my heart," I tell her all about Mara.

"I shut myself off from the outside world," I continue, my voice wavering with emotion. "Work became my refuge, my shield against the pain. I convinced myself that I didn't need anyone else, that solitude was the only way to heal."

As we stroll along the shoreline, memories flood my mind, vivid recollections of moments shared with Mara. I paint a picture of our life together, of the love we nurtured and the dreams we had woven. I speak of her infectious laughter, her gentle touch, and the way her eyes sparkled with joy. With each word, I can feel her presence, as if she's walking beside me, guiding me through this vulnerable confession.

"I built walls around my heart, Keisha," I confess, my voice thick with regret. "I didn't think I could ever love again, that the pain would forever define me. But meeting you, something shifted within me. It's as if you've reminded me of the beauty and possibility that life still holds."

Keisha listens intently, her gaze unwavering. I can sense the empathy radiating from her, as if she understands the complexities of grief and the struggle to find oneself amidst the ruins of loss. It's a rare connection, one that sparks hope within me, a flicker of light in the darkness.

We continue walking, our steps slow and deliberate, the sand warm beneath our feet. The conversation drifts to lighter topics, as if we've both acknowledged the weight of my past, yet choose to embrace the present moment. The ocean stretches out before us, vast and unyielding, mirroring the depths of my emotions.

As the sun begins to dip below the horizon, casting hues of orange and pink across the sky, I feel a sense of release, of catharsis. I've unburdened myself, allowing Keisha to witness the fragments of my shattered heart. In her presence, I find solace, a glimmer of hope that perhaps there is room for healing and love in my life once more.

We walk in silence for a while, the waves crashing against the shore, each rhythmic pulse serving as a reminder of the ebb and flow of life. The weight of my past still lingers, but in Keisha's company, I feel a newfound sense of possibility, as if the future holds the potential for healing and happiness.

As the sky darkens and the stars begin to twinkle above us, Keisha reaches out and gently takes my hand. Her touch is warm, grounding me in the present moment. It's a simple gesture, yet it carries a profound significance, a connection that transcends words.

"I'm grateful that you trusted me enough to share your story, Llanzo," Keisha says softly, her voice carrying a tenderness that resonates deep within me. "And I want you to know that I'm here for you."

As we continue our walk, the stars above twinkle with a radiance. Her words wash over me like a soothing balm, a salve for the wounds that have yet to heal.

The First Kiss

Keisha

It has been two days since Llanzo told me about Mara. Because of his work schedule, I hadn't seen him since, but we have spoken over the phone, so I am excited to get to spend the day with him. At 10 am we are meeting at the resort and we eat a late breakfast together.

As the morning sun casts a golden glow over the resort, I find myself seated across from Llanzo at a quaint outdoor cafe, the tantalizing aroma of freshly brewed coffee filling the air. We sip our beverages in comfortable silence, the gentle breeze carrying with it a sense of tranquility.

"So, how did you sleep?" I inquire, breaking the silence with a smile.

Llanzo looks at me, his eyes sparkling with a mix of emotions. "Better than I expected, Keisha," he replies, his voice carrying a hint of gratitude. "Opening up about Mara and sharing that part of my life with you was not easy, but it felt liberating.

44

Thank you for being there to listen."

I reach out and place my hand on his, offering a reassuring squeeze. "Llanzo, I'm here for you. It means a lot to me that you trust me enough to share your deepest sorrows and joys."

He nods appreciatively, a flicker of warmth crossing his face. "I never thought I would find someone who understands the complexities of my past, someone who sees beyond the surface. It's a rare gift, Keisha, and I'm grateful for our friendship."

I lean back in my chair, studying his face, filled with a mixture of admiration and curiosity. I reach across the table, intertwining my fingers with his. "Llanzo, I'm not asking you to forget Mara or to replace her. She will always hold a special place in your heart, and that's something I respect and honor."

A flicker of hope dances in his eyes, and he gives my hand a gentle squeeze. "Keisha, you have a way of making everything feel lighter, of bringing a sense of joy and warmth into my life."

I smile, feeling a sense of relief and excitement flood through me.

As we continue our breakfast, the weight of our pasts gradually lifts, replaced by a renewed sense of hope and possibility. We engage in lighthearted banter, sharing stories and dreams, savoring each moment of connection.

In that simple cafe, amidst the clinking of coffee cups and the gentle hum of conversation, we find solace in each other's presence. Our shared understanding and willingness to navigate the complexities of our individual journeys create a foundation of trust and love.

As we finish our breakfast, we rise from our seats, a newfound sense of anticipation and excitement filling the air. Hand in hand, we step into the day, ready to embrace the adventures that lie ahead, knowing that together, we can face whatever challenges come our way.

The sun shines brilliantly overhead as Llanzo and I make our way to the beach, hand in hand. The sand feels warm beneath my feet, a soothing contrast to the refreshing ocean breeze that sweeps through my hair. It's a perfect day—a day meant for basking in the sun's embrace and relishing in the company of someone special.

We spread out our towels on the sand, claiming a small piece of paradise for ourselves. Llanzo's eyes crinkle at the corners as he smiles, his gaze filled with a warmth that ignites a spark within me. We settle into a comfortable rhythm of conversation, sharing stories, dreams, and aspirations. With each passing moment, I find myself drawn further into his orbit, yearning to uncover the layers of his soul.

As the hours slip by, we immerse ourselves in the beauty of the beach, laughing, splashing in the waves, and building sandcastles like children. Llanzo's laughter is infectious, filling the air with a melody that lifts my spirits. It's in these simple moments, surrounded by the pristine beauty of nature, that I begin to see the depth of the connection we share.

As the sun descends towards the horizon, casting a golden hue across the sky, Llanzo suggests we take a sunset boat ride. The idea excites me, and I eagerly agree, curious to see where this adventure will lead. We board the boat, its gentle rocking lulling us into a state of tranquility. The warm colors of the sky reflect in the water, creating a canvas of breathtaking beauty.

As we glide through the gentle waves, the atmosphere is charged with an electric energy. We sit side by side, our shoulders brushing lightly, and a sense of anticipation hangs in the air. It's as if the universe is holding its breath, aware that something significant is about to unfold between us.

As the sun begins its descent, painting the sky in shades of fiery orange and dusky purple, Llanzo's hand finds mine, his fingers interlacing with mine as if seeking solace in our connection. The world around us seems to fade away, leaving only the two of us in this enchanted moment.

The boat comes to a gentle halt, and we find ourselves drifting in the embrace of the ocean. Llanzo turns towards me, his eyes searching mine, filled with a vulnerability that mirrors my own. Time slows, as if the universe is granting us this moment, this breathless pause before destiny takes hold.

And then, it happens—a whisper of a touch, the softest brush of lips against mine. In that instant, fireworks explode within me, igniting a flame that burns brighter than anything I've ever known. It's a kiss that speaks volumes, that conveys the depths of longing and desire we've both been holding back.

For a brief moment, I forget the world exists, lost in the intoxicating taste of possibility. But as reality begins to seep back in, I glimpse a flicker of doubt in Llanzo's eyes. It's a mix of longing and pain, a conflict that tugs at my heart. I sense his inner struggle, and my own emotions mirror his turmoil.

Before I can fully comprehend what is happening, the weight of his guilt crashes over me like a wave, drowning the burgeoning joy within me. Llanzo's expression changes, his face clouded with regret. It's as if he has stepped back into the shadows, locking away the vulnerability he had briefly revealed.

"I'm sorry," I whisper, my voice laced with confusion and hurt. "I didn't mean to overstep, to make you feel uncomfortable."

Llanzo's eyes meet mine, and his voice quivers with a mix of sorrow and regret. "No, Keisha, it's not you. It's me," he says, his words laden with a heaviness that resonates deep within my soul. "I feel like I just cheated on my wife, as if I've betrayed her memory. I'm not ready for anything more than being your friend, and I never want to hurt you."

His admission lands heavily on my heart, and I struggle to find the right words. The ache of unrequited emotions threatens to overwhelm me, but I know I must respect his journey, his need for healing. The bond we've formed is too precious to sacrifice on the altar of my desires.

Taking a deep breath, I reach out and gently cup Llanzo's face, my touch conveying understanding and acceptance. "Llanzo, I understand," I say, my voice filled with a mixture of sadness and admiration. "I don't want to push you into something you're not ready for. We can take things at your pace, and I'll be here for you, as a friend."

A mixture of relief and gratitude flashes across Llanzo's face, and he takes hold of my hand, his grip firm yet tender. We sit in silence, enveloped by the fading hues of the sunset, the waves lapping against the boat like a lullaby. In that moment, a new understanding is born—a delicate balance of affection and restraint, of cherishing the present while honoring the past.

As the boat glides back towards the shore, we find solace in each other's presence. We may have taken a step back from the precipice of romance, but our connection remains unbroken, a beacon of warmth and support in the tumultuous sea of emotions.

We navigate our evolving dynamic with grace, cherishing the moments of laughter and companionship. Our friendship deepens, woven with shared experiences and heartfelt conversations. And though a part of me still longs for more, I find solace in the knowledge that time has its own way of healing wounds and transforming hearts.

As the sun sets, I am reminded that love takes many forms

and unfolds at its own pace. The first kiss may have signaled the beginning of a new chapter, but it also serves as a poignant reminder of the complexities of healing and the resilience of the human spirit. And so, with hope in my heart, I embrace the uncertainty of what lies ahead, grateful for the connection I've found with Llanzo, and open to the possibilities that await us on this journey called life.

Keisha's Inner Conflict

Keisha

The next day, I can't seem to get the kiss we shared out of my mind. I was having a whirlwind of emotions swirls within me, each one vying for dominance as I navigate the labyrinth of my heart. I never expected to meet someone like Llanzo during my sabbatical, and yet, here he is, a captivating presence that stirs something deep within me. But as the days pass, I find myself caught in a tumultuous storm of conflicting desires and uncertainties.

Part of me wants to surrender to the enchantment that Llanzo weaves around me. His smile, his touch, the way he makes me feel alive—it's a temptation I struggle to resist. I can't deny the growing connection between us, the way my heart skips a beat when he's near, or the warmth that spreads through me with his every word. But another part of me, the rational voice in the depths of my mind, warns of the consequences that lie ahead.

I'm on a sabbatical, a break from the demands and responsibilities of my life back home. It was meant to be a time of self-discovery, of recharging my weary spirit. Getting involved with someone, especially someone as complex as Llanzo, feels like a contradiction to the purpose of this journey. How can I truly find myself when I'm entangled in the web of newfound emotions?

Moreover, the knowledge that Llanzo isn't ready for any kind of relationship adds fuel to the fire of my inner conflict. He carries the weight of his past, the loss of his wife, and the guilt that gnaws at his conscience. I understand his hesitation, his need for healing, but it adds another layer of complexity to the choices I must make.

I find solace in the vast expanse of the ocean, its ebb and flow mirroring the shifting tides of my emotions. Each wave crashes against the shore, as if washing away the remnants of my doubts and fears. But the undertow of desire remains, a constant reminder of the path I've yet to tread.

There are moments when I catch myself daydreaming, lost in fantasies of what could be. Imagining a future where Llanzo and I explore the depths of our connection, where we conquer our fears and find solace in each other's arms. It's intoxicating, this dream of a love that transcends time and circumstances. Yet, I'm brought back to reality with a jolt, my dreams colliding with the stark truth that lies before me.

I confide in the gentle sway of the hammock, seeking its wisdom as I pour out my thoughts and doubts. The wind rustles through the palm trees, as if whispering secrets of its own. It reminds me that life is a tapestry of moments, woven together by choices both big and small. And in this moment, the choice lies in my hands—do I surrender to the allure of love or do I retreat into the safety of solitude?

The answer eludes me, dancing just beyond my grasp. Fear and longing intertwine, their dance echoing the intricate steps of a delicate waltz. I want to dive headfirst into the sea of possibilities, to embrace the unknown and trust in the magic of love. But the practical voice within me whispers caution, urging me to guard my heart and preserve the sanctuary of my sabbatical.

I seek solace in the company of the written word, losing myself in the pages of novels that transport me to different worlds. The stories of love and heartbreak resonate deeply, reminding me that no journey towards love is without its trials and tribulations. Perhaps, like the heroines of those tales, I too must find the courage to confront my fears, to take a leap of faith despite the uncertainties that lie ahead.

In the depths of my inner conflict, I realize that the answers I seek cannot be found solely within myself. I need clarity, guidance, and perspective. And so, I seek the wisdom of those who have walked similar paths, who have weathered the storms of their own hearts.

Later that day, as the sun sets in a blaze of fiery colors, I find myself sitting with Llanzo on the porch of his beachfront home. The air is heavy with anticipation, the quietude broken only by the distant sound of crashing waves. We sit in companionable silence, our eyes drawn to the horizon as if searching for answers in the vast expanse of the ocean.

With a deep breath, I gather the courage to break the silence that has settled between us. "Llanzo," I begin, my voice tinged with vulnerability, "I'm struggling with my feelings for you. It's hard for me to reconcile the desire I feel with the knowledge that you're not ready for anything more."

Llanzo's gaze meets mine, and I see a mixture of understanding and regret flicker across his features. He takes my hand in his, his touch both comforting and electrifying. "Keisha," he says, his voice soft yet resolute, "I won't deny that I feel a deep connection with you, but I can't ignore the pain and guilt that still linger within me. I don't want to lead you on or hurt you in any way."

Tears well up in my eyes, a mixture of frustration and affection. "I appreciate your honesty, Llanzo," I reply, my voice filled with a mix of gratitude and sadness. "But what does this mean for us? Can we continue to explore our connection while respecting the boundaries you need?"

Llanzo's expression softens, his thumb gently caressing the back of my hand. "Keisha, I care about you deeply," he says, his voice filled with sincerity. "I don't want to let go of the bond we've formed. We can take things slow, be there for each other, and see where this journey takes us. But I need you to understand that I may still have moments of doubt and hesitation."

His words bring a sense of relief and hope, a glimmer of possibility amidst the turmoil of my emotions. I realize that our connection is not black and white, but a myriad of shades that demand patience and understanding. We may not have all the answers now, but we can navigate this delicate dance together, allowing our hearts to guide us.

As the night sky blankets us in its starry embrace, I lean my head against Llanzo's shoulder, finding solace in his presence. In this moment, I choose to embrace the uncertainty, to surrender to the unfolding chapters of our story. It may not be a traditional love story, but it's a tale of resilience, growth, and the power of connection.

With renewed determination, I take a deep breath, ready

to embrace the journey ahead. The inner conflict that once consumed me begins to dissipate, replaced by a sense of serenity and acceptance. I am no longer torn between the desire for love and the need for solitude. Instead, I choose to honor both sides of myself, allowing them to coexist harmoniously.

As the waves continue their eternal dance along the shore, I realize that life, like the ocean, is ever-changing. And in this moment, I am content to let the tides carry me, trusting that the path I've chosen will lead me to where I'm meant to be.

Learning About Llanzo's Business

Llanzo

As Keisha and I step into the small, quaint beachside cafe, a sense of calm washes over us, like a gentle caress from the ocean breeze. The interior of the cafe beckons us with its warm, inviting ambiance, setting the stage for a moment of tranquility amidst the bustling world.

Wooden floors, weathered by time, lead us to a table nestled by the window, offering a breathtaking view of the azure expanse stretching out before us. The sunlight pours in, casting a golden glow that illuminates our surroundings with a touch of magic. The walls, adorned with vibrant paintings of the ocean's beauty, bring a splash of color to the serene atmosphere.

Taking our seats, we sink into cushioned chairs, feeling the weight of the world lift off our shoulders. The gentle lapping of waves serenades our conversation, harmonizing with the soft melody playing in the background. We find solace in the intimate space, as if the outside world has faded away, leaving only the two of us in this oasis of serenity.

The aroma of freshly brewed coffee dances in the air, mingling with the salty tang of the sea. As we exchange glances, a shared smile reflects the anticipation of savoring the simple pleasures that lie ahead. Our fingers interlace, connecting us in a bond of warmth and affection.

The menu presents an array of culinary delights, tantalizing our taste buds with the flavors of the island. From succulent seafood caught that very morning to exotic fruits bursting with tropical sweetness, each dish promises an adventure for the senses. We embark on a journey of exploration, eagerly sampling the vibrant colors and delectable aromas that grace our plates.

Engrossed in conversation, our voices blend harmoniously with the soothing sounds of the cafe. Laughter mingles with the clinking of glasses, creating a symphony of joy and camaraderie. In this shared moment, the outside world seems distant, its worries and demands momentarily forgotten.

As we gaze out through the window, the panorama before us captivates our attention. The waves crash against the shore with a rhythmic cadence, a testament to the eternal dance of the ocean. The sun casts its golden glow upon the water, transforming it into a shimmering canvas of liquid gold.

With each sip of coffee, the rich flavors awaken our senses, amplifying the connection between us. We share stories, dreams, and aspirations, finding comfort in the openness of our hearts. The cafe becomes a sanctuary, where time stands still, and the weight of the world is replaced by a profound sense of peace.

I can't help but feel a surge of pride as I talk about my excursion company. The passion that fuels my every endeavor bubbles up within me, eager to be shared with someone who has come to mean so much to me.

"Keisha," I begin, my voice filled with enthusiasm, "let me tell you about my business. It's more than just taking tourists on excursions—it's about showcasing the true beauty of Jamaica, the wonders that lie beneath its surface and within its vibrant culture."

Her eyes sparkle with curiosity, a genuine interest shining through. "Llanzo, I'd love to hear all about it. Your passion is infectious."

I take a moment to gather my thoughts, a mix of memories and dreams colliding in my mind. "You see," I continue, my voice laced with nostalgia, "growing up on this island, I was always captivated by its natural wonders—the crystal-clear waters, the lush greenery, the vibrant coral reefs. It felt like a hidden treasure, waiting to be discovered."

Keisha leans forward, her gaze fixed on me, urging me to continue. "So, I made it my mission to share this treasure with the world. I started my excursion company to offer visitors a chance to explore the unspoiled beauty of Jamaica, to witness its majesty firsthand."

I take a sip of my coffee, the rich aroma filling my senses, before continuing. "Every excursion we offer is carefully crafted to showcase the unique wonders of this island. Whether it's snorkeling with reef sharks, diving into underwater caves, or hiking through lush rainforests, each experience is designed to create unforgettable memories."

As I speak, memories of past excursions come rushing back—the laughter of families as they spot colorful fish, the awe in the eyes of newlyweds as they witness a breathtaking sunset from a secluded beach, the sheer joy of children as they discover the wonders of the underwater world for the first time. These moments fuel my passion, reminding me of the impact our company has on people's lives.

"But it's not just about the activities," I explain, a hint of emotion creeping into my voice. "It's about fostering a deep connection with Jamaica, its people, and its culture. We take great care in partnering with local communities, supporting their livelihoods and sharing their stories with our guests. From sampling traditional Jamaican cuisine to immersing ourselves in the vibrant music and dance, we aim to create a truly immersive experience."

Keisha's eyes light up, her curiosity piqued. "Llanzo, it sounds incredible. I can feel the love and dedication you pour into every aspect of your business. What drives you? What keeps you going?"

A smile tugs at the corners of my lips as I contemplate her question. "Keisha, it's the joy I see in people's eyes, the spark of wonder and appreciation for the natural beauty that surrounds us. It's the knowledge that through our excursions, we're not only showing visitors the magnificence of Jamaica, but also instilling a sense of respect and responsibility towards the environment."

I pause for a moment, the weight of my words sinking in. "You see, this island has given me so much. It's a place that holds my fondest memories, but it's also a place that faces challenges—environmental degradation, the impact of tourism, and more. By showcasing its beauty and fostering a deep appreciation for its delicate ecosystems, I hope to inspire others to become stewards of this land."

Keisha's gaze softens, a deep understanding passing between us. She reaches across the table, her hand finding mine, and I feel a connection that goes beyond words.

"Llanzo," she says, her voice filled with warmth, "your passion for this island and its people is truly inspiring. I can see why you've dedicated yourself to sharing its beauty with the world. It's not just about the excursions; it's about making a difference, creating awareness, and fostering a love for this place."

Her words resonate deeply within me, affirming the purpose that drives me each day. The weight of my responsibility as a custodian of Jamaica's natural wonders feels both humbling and empowering.

As the sun begins its descent, casting a fiery glow across the horizon, we sit in comfortable silence, the sounds of the waves providing a soothing backdrop to our thoughts. In this moment, I realize that Keisha not only understands my passion, but she embraces it, supporting me in my mission to showcase the beauty of Jamaica.

I reach out and gently squeeze her hand, a silent gesture of gratitude. "Keisha, thank you for listening, for understanding the essence of what I do. Your presence in my life has brought an added sense of purpose and joy."

A soft smile graces her lips, and her eyes meet mine with a depth of understanding. "Llanzo, I believe in you and the impact you're making. Together, we can continue to inspire others and make a difference in the world."

In that moment, as the sun dips below the horizon, I am filled with a renewed sense of hope. As we sit there, the fading light painting the sky in shades of pink and orange. The bond between us grows stronger, our shared dreams intertwining, as we revel in the magic of this island paradise.

As the night settles in, we rise from our seats, our hearts filled with anticipation for the adventures that await us. We walk along the moonlit beach, ready to embrace the challenges and triumphs that lie ahead. And with each step, the echoes of our shared purpose resonate in harmony with the gentle lapping of the waves. We continue to weave our stories into the fabric of Jamaica.

A Night Out

❧❧❧

Keisha

As the sun begins to set, casting a warm golden glow over the city, Llanzo and I embark on a thrilling journey through Montego Bay's vibrant nightlife. The air is filled with anticipation and excitement as we step into the rhythmic pulse of the city's streets.

We find ourselves immersed in the heart of the entertainment district, where the neon lights of clubs and bars illuminate the night sky. Laughter and music intertwine, creating an electric atmosphere that permeates every corner. The streets are alive with the sounds of reggae, dancehall, and calypso, enticing us to follow the melodies that beckon from beyond.

Llanzo's hand clasps mine, grounding me amidst the whirlwind of sights and sounds. We navigate through the bustling crowd, the warmth of his touch providing a comforting anchor as we make our way towards a vibrant open-air bar that emanates an irresistible energy. The scent of rum and the lively

61

melodies of live music entice us, drawing us closer to the heart of the celebration.

We step into the bar, and the vibrant energy envelops us. The air is infused with the intoxicating aromas of tropical cocktails and spicy delicacies. The bar is a kaleidoscope of colors, with bright umbrellas casting playful shadows over the patrons. The sound of laughter and animated conversations fills the air, blending harmoniously with the pulsating rhythms.

We find a cozy spot at the bar, perched on cushioned stools, immersing ourselves in the ambiance. The bartenders, adorned with colorful shirts and infectious smiles, expertly mix cocktails that showcase the exotic flavors of the island. I'm enticed by the array of options, from classic rum punches to innovative creations infused with local fruits and spices.

Llanzo and I engage in lively conversation, our voices rising above the music. We share stories, dreams, and anecdotes, each word deepening our connection. The vibrant energy of the crowd fuels our enthusiasm, and we can't help but be swept away by the contagious joy that permeates the atmosphere.

The music beckons us, and we decide to leave the confines of the bar and venture onto the dance floor. The vibrant beats envelop us, the rhythm pulsating through our bodies. We sway, we groove, and we surrender ourselves to the freedom of movement. The dance floor becomes our sanctuary, a place where time slows down and all worries dissipate.

Llanzo's skilled movements mirror mine, our bodies moving in harmony to the infectious rhythms. His touch sends electric currents through me, igniting a fire that blazes with each step. Together, we become part of a collective dance, a symphony of bodies expressing themselves through the universal language of music.

The night progresses, and we venture deeper into the vibrant heart of Montego Bay. We explore hidden gems and stumble upon intimate venues where local musicians captivate our hearts with soul-stirring melodies. The music carries us on a journey, evoking emotions that run deep within our souls. We sway, we sing, and we embrace the beauty of the moment.

The city's rich culinary tapestry invites us to indulge in its flavors. We visit street food stalls, where the tantalizing aroma of jerk chicken, savory patties, and fresh seafood fills the air. We delight in the explosion of spices on our tongues, savoring the authenticity and vibrancy of Jamaican cuisine.

As the night unfolds, we find solace in a secluded beachside bar, where the crashing waves provide a soothing backdrop to our intimate conversation. The moon casts its gentle glow over the water, creating a serene and romantic ambiance. We share secrets, dreams, and vulnerabilities, feeling the walls around our hearts crumble with each word spoken.

In this moment, as the laughter and conversations blend with the soothing sound of the waves, I feel a sense of serenity and contentment wash over me. Llanzo's presence is a calming force, his deep gaze and genuine smile reassuring me that this night is something special.

We talk about our passions, our dreams, and the journeys that have led us to this very point in time. Llanzo's words resonate with a profound appreciation for his roots, his love for Jamaica evident in every story he shares. He speaks of his desire to showcase the beauty of his homeland, to offer visitors an authentic and transformative experience.

His eyes light up as he describes the vibrant coral reefs, the lush rainforests, and the cascading waterfalls that adorn the island. He paints a vivid picture of the crystal-clear waters teeming with colorful fish, the sun-kissed beaches inviting you to bask in their warmth. I can almost feel the cool breeze caressing my skin as he recounts his adventures exploring hidden coves and secluded spots that only locals know of.

As Llanzo speaks, his passion is contagious, igniting a desire within me to experience the wonders he describes firsthand. His genuine love for his work and his commitment to sharing the beauty of Jamaica with others is both inspiring and humbling. I can't help but admire his dedication and the joy he finds in connecting people with nature and culture.

Amidst the backdrop of the gentle lapping waves and the distant laughter of fellow beachgoers, I realize that this night is more than just a night out. It is a glimpse into the depths of Llanzo's soul, a window into his dreams and aspirations. And as I listen intently to his stories, I can't help but feel a deep sense of connection and admiration for the man before me.

As the night unfolds and we find ourselves in the cozy ambiance of the beachside bar, the sound of the waves creating a soothing backdrop, Llanzo and I engage in a conversation that flows effortlessly, like a gentle current guiding us deeper into connection. Savoring the last moments of this enchanting evening. The sky is studded with twinkling stars, a breathtaking display that mirrors the sparkle in our eyes.

I take a sip of my tropical cocktail, the fruity flavors exploding on my tongue, as I turn to Llanzo with a curious smile. "Tell me more about your excursion company. What inspired you to start it?"

Llanzo's eyes light up with passion, a spark of excitement dancing within them. He takes a moment to collect his thoughts before answering, his voice filled with warmth. "You see, Keisha, growing up in Jamaica, I've always been captivated by the beauty that surrounds us. The pristine beaches, the vibrant coral reefs, the lush mountains. It's a treasure trove of natural wonders."

He pauses for a moment, gazing out at the ocean as if drawing inspiration from its vastness. "I wanted to share this beauty with the world, to give people an authentic experience of Jamaica. Not just the tourist hotspots, but the hidden gems that make our island so special."

I lean forward, captivated by his words. "That sounds incredible. So, what kind of experiences do you offer?"

Llanzo's smile widens, his enthusiasm infectious. "We offer a range of experiences that allow visitors to truly immerse themselves in the heart and soul of Jamaica. From snorkeling adventures in the crystal-clear waters to hiking through the rainforests, we strive to create meaningful connections with nature and our vibrant culture."

He takes a moment to take in the atmosphere around us, his eyes glimmering with nostalgia. "One of my favorite experiences is taking people to explore the coral reefs while snorkeling. It's like entering a whole new world beneath the waves. The vibrant colors of the fish, the graceful movements of the sea turtles, and the awe-inspiring beauty of the coral formations... It's a breathtaking sight."

I can't help but be drawn into his vivid descriptions, imagining myself diving into the depths of the ocean alongside him. "That sounds absolutely amazing. I've always been fascinated by marine life. It must be a truly transformative experience."

Llanzo nods, his gaze locking with mine. "It is, Keisha. There's something about being in the presence of such natural wonders that fills your heart with a sense of awe and gratitude. It reminds you of the vastness of our world and the importance of preserving these precious ecosystems."

I can't help but admire Llanzo's dedication to preserving the beauty of his homeland. His words resonate deeply within me, igniting a desire to explore and connect with nature in a profound way. "It's truly inspiring what you're doing, Llanzo. I can sense the love and passion you have for Jamaica and sharing its wonders with others."

A soft smile graces Llanzo's face, his eyes shimmering with appreciation. "Thank you, Keisha. It's a labor of love, and I couldn't imagine doing anything else. Seeing the smiles on people's faces and witnessing their genuine awe makes it all worthwhile."

As our conversation continues, we delve deeper into the intricacies of his excursion company, discussing the logistics, the challenges, and the rewarding moments. With each word exchanged, our connection grows stronger, a tapestry of shared dreams and shared love for the beauty that surrounds us.

In this intimate setting, amidst the gentle whispers of the ocean and the flickering candlelight, I feel a sense of belonging and gratitude for the serendipitous encounter that brought Llanzo into my life. Little do I know that this night will be etched in my memory as a pivotal moment, forever.

Walking away from the beachside bar, I carry with me a renewed sense of purpose and an appreciation for the beauty that surrounds us. Llanzo's passion has awakened something within me, a desire to seek out my own adventures and embrace the magic of life. And as I make my way back, the memories of this unforgettable night dance in my mind, fueling my spirit and reminding me of the possibilities that lie ahead.

Llanzo's Confession

Llanzo

As the sun sets over the horizon, casting a warm, golden glow on the tranquil beach, I find myself walking hand in hand with Keisha, the rhythmic sound of the waves providing a soothing soundtrack to our footsteps. There's an undeniable sense of anticipation in the air, as if the very universe is holding its breath, waiting for the words that are about to spill from my lips.

We come to a stop at a secluded spot, where the sand meets the water, creating a picturesque backdrop for the emotions swirling within me. I turn to Keisha, her eyes shimmering with curiosity and a hint of apprehension. Taking a deep breath, I gather my thoughts, my heart pounding in my chest.

"Keisha," I begin, my voice laced with a mixture of vulnerability and determination, "there's something I need to confess to you."

Her gaze locks with mine, her features a canvas of emotions.

I can see the flicker of uncertainty, but also a glimmer of hope dancing in her eyes. She nods, encouraging me to continue.

"Ever since you came into my life, Keisha, everything has changed," I confess, my voice steady but filled with raw emotion. "You've brought light into the darkest corners of my heart, awakening feelings that I thought were long buried."

A soft breeze caresses our faces, as if nature itself is whispering its approval, urging me to lay bare the depths of my soul. I reach out to gently brush a strand of hair behind her ear, my touch filled with tenderness.

"I want you to know that I've spent the past two years shutting myself off from the world, living in the shadows of grief and guilt," I continue, my voice trembling ever so slightly. "But being with you, Keisha, has shown me that it's possible to move on, to embrace the beauty that life still has to offer."

Her eyes widen with a mixture of surprise and anticipation, a flicker of hope igniting within her. I take a moment to gather my thoughts, wanting to choose my words carefully, to convey the depth of my feelings.

"Keisha, I've fallen in love with you," I finally admit, my voice filled with a blend of awe and certainty. "I never thought I'd be ready to open my heart again, to let someone new in. But being with you, it feels right. It feels like destiny."

Tears shimmer in her eyes, glistening like tiny diamonds in the fading sunlight. I reach out to wipe away a tear that escapes, my touch gentle and filled with reverence. Her hand finds its way to my cheek, her touch warm and comforting.

With a mix of trepidation and anticipation, I take a step closer to Keisha, our breaths mingling in the salty sea breeze. "Keisha, I understand if you need time to process all of this," I say softly, my voice filled with a mix of hope and understanding. "I don't expect to have all the answers right now. But I wanted to be honest with you, to let you know that my feelings are real, and I'm willing to take this journey with you, one step at a time."

Her eyes search mine, a swirl of emotions dancing within them. I see the flicker of vulnerability, the flicker of longing, and a hint of something else—a glimmer of possibility. She takes a deep breath, her voice steady but filled with a touch of uncertainty.

"Llanzo, this is all so unexpected. You know how I feel about you and I wasn't sure you would ever feel the same about me," she confesses, her words a gentle affirmation. "I'm willing to explore to see where our hearts lead us."

A wave of relief washes over me, a sense of gratitude filling every fiber of my being. I reach out to gently take her hand in mine, our fingers intertwining like two puzzle pieces finding their perfect match. "Keisha, I know that together, we'll embark on this journey, cherishing every moment filled with love, understanding, and shared dreams."

We stand there, on the precipice of something beautiful, the world around us fading into the background as our hearts beat in unison. The moon rises in the night sky, casting a soft glow on our intertwined hands, a symbol of the connection that has been forged.

The night is bathed in a soft, ethereal glow as Keisha and I find ourselves standing on the deserted beach, the rhythm of the crashing waves creating a symphony of serenity. The air is charged with anticipation, as if the universe itself is holding its breath, aware of the momentousness of what is about to transpire.

Our gazes meet, locked in a timeless exchange of unspoken desires and longing. In the hushed silence that surrounds us,

I see the reflection of my own feelings mirrored in Keisha's eyes. There's a vulnerability and a yearning, a silent plea for connection and a shared understanding of the depths of our hearts.

Slowly, almost instinctively, our bodies gravitate towards each other, drawn by an invisible force that has woven its way through our souls. I reach out, my hand trembling slightly, to gently cup Keisha's cheek, my touch feather-light and tender. Her eyes flutter closed, surrendering to the moment, her lips parting ever so slightly.

In that fleeting second, time seems to suspend, the world fading into the background as our hearts beat in synchrony. The space between us narrows until there is no distance left to bridge. Our lips meet, a gentle collision of warmth and tenderness that sends a shiver down my spine.

It is a kiss filled with a myriad of emotions—passion, longing, and a profound connection that defies words. In that tender union of our mouths, I taste the sweetness of possibility, the intoxicating blend of vulnerability and desire that blooms between us.

The world around us fades into insignificance as we become lost in the moment, our bodies pressed against each other, our souls intertwining. With each gentle caress of our lips, the weight of our pasts and the uncertainties of our future melt away, leaving only the intoxicating present.

Time seems to both stretch and contract, as if this single kiss contains a lifetime of promises and unspoken vows. It is a moment of surrender and revelation, where two souls lay bare their vulnerabilities and open their hearts to the boundless potential of love.

As the kiss deepens, our breaths mingle, creating a delicate dance of shared breath and whispered sighs. It is as if our very beings have merged, the boundaries that once separated us dissolving into nothingness. In that embrace, I feel the weight of Keisha's trust and the power of her love, igniting a fire within me that burns brighter than any I have ever known.

But as our lips part, I catch a glimpse of uncertainty flickering in Keisha's eyes. A mix of emotions swirls within me—hope, fear, and the unwavering desire to protect her heart. I take her face in my hands, my voice filled with sincerity as I speak the words that lie heavy on my tongue.

We continue along the moonlit shore, the waves serenade us with their rhythmic melody, echoing the symphony of our hearts. In the embrace of the night, we share whispers of dreams and aspirations, weaving our souls together with each word exchanged. It is a night that will forever be etched in our memories, a pivotal moment that marks the beginning of an extraordinary love story.

The world around us seems to come alive, brimming with vibrant colors and hidden possibilities. With each passing moment, our connection deepens, unveiling layers of shared laughter, shared tears, and shared experiences. Together, we explore the depths of our beings, unraveling the intricacies of our pasts and envisioning a future filled with boundless love and unwavering support.

As the stars twinkle overhead, casting their gentle glow upon us, I am overwhelmed by a profound sense of gratitude. Gratitude for the serendipitous encounter that brought Keisha into my life, for the courage to embrace vulnerability, and for the shared moments that are yet to come. We may have stumbled upon love unexpectedly, but it is a gift that we are both willing to cherish and nurture.

In the softness of the night, with the ocean as our witness, we walk hand in hand, guided by the strength of our connection and the promise of a love that defies all odds. With every step we take, I am filled with a sense of wonder and awe, grateful for the opportunity to embark on this remarkable journey with Keisha by my side.

We stand outside her door, bathed in the soft glow of the moonlight, time seems to suspend around us. Our lips meet in a tender and lingering kiss, a testament to the connection that has grown between us. In that single moment, I can feel the weight of our emotions, the unspoken promises that pass between us with every touch of our lips.

Our kiss deepens, I can sense the longing in her eyes, mirrored by the desire that courses through my veins. The unspoken invitation hangs in the air, silently beckoning me to step into her world, to stay a little longer and immerse ourselves in the warmth of our love. I can see it in her eyes, the longing to have me by her side, to share this night and countless more to come.

She fumbles for her keys, her eyes never leaving mine, and I can sense the hesitation in her movements. The unspoken question lingers between us, challenging us to step beyond the boundaries of the present moment. The door swings open, and we find ourselves faced with a choice - to part ways, succumbing to the rationality of the situation, or to surrender to the powerful current of our desires.

In that moment, as I look into her eyes, I know that the decision has already been made. The magnetic pull between us is too strong to resist. We step inside the sanctuary of her room, closing the door behind us, as the world outside fades away, leaving only the two of us in this intimate space.

The air is thick with anticipation as our bodies gravitate towards each other. The gentle brush of her fingertips against my cheek sends shivers down my spine, igniting a fire within me that can no longer be contained. Our lips meet once again, this time with an intensity fueled by desire, a craving to taste the depths of our connection.

As our clothes fall away, piece by piece, revealing the vulnerability of our bare souls, the room fills with a sense of raw passion. Every touch, every caress, is an expression of our love, an affirmation of the bond that has formed between us. In the embrace of each other's bodies, we find solace and ecstasy, lost in a world where time ceases to exist.

With every whisper of our names, every sigh that escapes our lips, we surrender to the rhythm of our desires, dancing in perfect harmony. Our bodies intertwine, creating a symphony of pleasure, as we explore the depths of our love with a reverence that surpasses physicality. Each movement, each sensation, is imbued with an overwhelming sense of tenderness and adoration.

In the aftermath of our union, we lay intertwined, our bodies drenched in a sheen of sweat, our breaths intermingling. Our eyes lock, and in that silent exchange, we know that this moment is not just about physical gratification, but about the sacred connection we share. It is a testament to the depth of our love, an affirmation that we are meant to walk this journey together.

As we lay there, basking in the afterglow of our love, I am filled with a profound sense of gratitude. Gratitude for the serendipity that brought us together, for the courage to follow our hearts, and for the unspoken promises we have made to each other. In this intimate space, I realize that our love is a force that transcends time and circumstance, a love that has the power to heal and transform us both.

As the night draws on, we find solace in each other's arms, knowing that the dawn will bring new adventures and challenges. But for now, in this sacred sanctuary of love, we revel in the beauty of our connection, cherishing every moment as if time itself stands still. Wrapped in the warmth of our embrace, I know that this night has etched itself into the tapestry of our lives, becoming a cherished memory that will forever be etched in our hearts.

I press my lips against her forehead, savoring the delicate touch of her skin against mine. The room is filled with an ethereal glow, as if the universe itself is celebrating our union. In this moment, there are no words needed, for our souls speak a language that transcends mere words. We find solace in the quietude, in the gentle rise and fall of our breaths, as we bask in the afterglow of our lovemaking.

As our bodies intertwine in a tender embrace, I am overwhelmed by a profound sense of contentment. In Keisha's arms, I find refuge from the storm that once consumed me, a sanctuary where I am free to love and be loved. She has become my anchor, guiding me towards a future brimming with hope and possibilities.

In the gentle lull of the night, I watch as she surrenders to the embrace of sleep, her features softened by the tranquility that washes over her. I trace the contours of her face with my fingertips, memorizing every curve, every delicate line, committing it to memory like a painter etching the portrait of his muse.

As I lay there beside her, I am filled with a sense of awe and wonder. How did I come to deserve such a profound connection? How did I find someone whose presence illuminates my world with such brilliance? It is a question that lingers in the depths of my soul, but I know that sometimes, love is not meant to be understood, but rather to be embraced and cherished.

As the night unfurls its tapestry of stars outside the window, I am reminded of the vastness of the universe and the infinitesimal beauty of our love. In this moment, there is no past or future, only the sacredness of the present, as we lie entwined, two souls bound by an unbreakable bond.

I press a gentle kiss to her lips, whispering words of love into the stillness of the room. In this sanctuary of love, I am filled with a sense of gratitude for the journey that has led us here, for the trials and tribulations that have shaped us into the people we are today. And as I close my eyes, feeling her warmth against my skin, I know that this love is a gift, a rare and precious treasure that I will cherish for all eternity.

A Jamaican Adventure

Kiesha

The morning sun paints the sky in hues of gold and tangerine as Llanzo and I embark on our Jamaican adventure. With a sense of excitement bubbling within me, I can't help but feel grateful for the opportunity to explore this vibrant island alongside the man who has captured my heart.

As we drive along the winding coastal road, the lush greenery of Jamaica envelops us. The air is alive with the sweet scent of tropical flowers and the rhythmic chirping of exotic birds. The road leads us to a hidden gem, a secluded waterfall nestled amidst the emerald foliage.

The moment we step out of the car, I'm captivated by the raw beauty that surrounds us. I walk side by side with Llanzo as we embark on our Jamaican adventure, ready to explore the hidden gems of this beautiful island. The air is filled with anticipation, and our hearts beat in sync with the rhythm of excitement. We venture off the beaten path, eager to discover the less-traveled parts of Jamaica that hold the promise of untouched natural wonders.

As we make our way to a secluded waterfall nestled within a lush rainforest, the sound of cascading water grows louder with each step. The emerald foliage envelops us, creating a sense of enchantment. I turn to Llanzo, my eyes sparkling with curiosity. "Can you imagine the power and beauty of this waterfall, Llanzo? It's as if nature itself is putting on a mesmerizing show just for us."

He smiles, his eyes reflecting the same wonder. "It's truly breathtaking, Keisha. This is the kind of place that reminds us of the immense beauty that exists in the world, and how fortunate we are to witness it together."

We reach the edge of the waterfall, the water crashing down with a resounding roar. I can feel the mist kissing my skin, refreshing and invigorating. Llanzo takes my hand, and we stand there in awe, letting the moment wash over us. "This is nature's masterpiece," I whisper, my voice filled with reverence. "It reminds me of the power of love, how it can be both gentle and fierce, just like the water cascading before us."

Llanzo's gaze never leaves mine, his voice filled with tenderness. "You're right, Keisha. Love has its own ebb and flow, just like the waters of this waterfall. It can be gentle and nurturing, or passionate and invigorating. And in this moment, as we stand here together, I can't help but feel that our love is as boundless as the waterfall itself."

Leaving the waterfall behind, we continue our journey, venturing towards a hidden beach known only to the locals. It is untouched by the crowds of tourists. The path is lined with vibrant flowers, their petals painting the landscape with a kaleidoscope of colors. As we step onto the soft sand it is warm and soft like powdered sugar beneath our feet. The azure waves crashing against the shore, I can't help but gasp at the beauty that surrounds us. The water stretches out before us, merging seamlessly with the horizon.

We find solace in the solitude of these secluded beaches, reveling in the feeling of being the only souls on this stretch of paradise. Hand in hand, we stroll along the shoreline, our footprints washed away by the gentle caress of the tide. The salty breeze tousles our hair, carrying with it the whispers of untold stories.

As we explore the hidden nooks and crannies of these beaches, we stumble upon tide pools teeming with vibrant sea creatures. Llanzo bends down, carefully picking up a starfish and placing it in my palm. Its delicate texture and vibrant hues captivate me, a reminder of the intricate beauty that lies beneath the surface.

Llanzo takes my hand and we walk along the shoreline, the warm sand embracing our feet. "Keisha, look at the ocean," he says, his voice filled with awe. "It's as if the entire world is reflected in its vastness. This is a reminder that our love is just a small part of something greater, something that connects us to everything around us."

I gaze out at the endless expanse of the sea, feeling a sense of unity with the universe. "Llanzo, you're right. This moment reminds me of the infinite possibilities that lie ahead for us, and the vastness of the love we have for each other. It's as if the waves themselves carry our hopes and dreams, whispering promises of a future filled with joy and adventure."

We sit down on the beach, our fingers interlaced as we watch the sun begin its descent. The sky transforms into a canvas of vibrant hues, the warm oranges and pinks blending with the cool blues. The world around us seems to quiet down, as if nature itself is holding its breath, waiting for the perfect moment to unveil its masterpiece.

"Llanzo," I say softly, my voice filled with gratitude. "This sunset is a reflection of our love, a kaleidoscope of colors that mirrors the depth and beauty we have found in each other."

We spend hours basking in the sun, building sandcastles, and letting the waves tickle our toes. The world seems to fade away, leaving only the two of us in this idyllic haven. With each passing moment, my connection with Llanzo deepens, intertwining our souls like the roots of a sturdy Jamaican tree.

We walk back to the waterfall and it cascades down in a mesmerizing display, its waters glistening like liquid diamonds under the sunlight. Llanzo takes my hand, leading me towards the pool at the base of the falls.

We wade into the crystal-clear water, its coolness enveloping us, rejuvenating our spirits. The sensation of tiny droplets caressing my skin is both invigorating and soothing. We laugh and splash, feeling like carefree children as we embrace the playful energy of the moment.

Llanzo's eyes sparkle with delight as he points out vibrant fish darting among the rocks beneath the water's surface. Their vibrant colors create a kaleidoscope of beauty, a testament to the diversity of marine life that thrives in these waters. We watch in awe as the fish weave through the currents, their graceful movements a dance of nature.

He turns to me, his eyes filled with warmth and love. "Keisha, every color in this sunset reminds me of the vibrant spectrum of emotions that you've brought into my life. From the fiery passion of the oranges and reds to the tranquil serenity of the blues and purples, it all reflects the depth and richness of our connection."

I lean closer to him, feeling the soft caress of the breeze on my skin. "Llanzo, being here with you, witnessing this stunning sunset, I can't help but feel an overwhelming sense of gratitude for the love we share. It's a love that ignites my soul and fills every fiber of my being with joy."

As the sun sinks lower on the horizon, casting a golden glow across the beach, Llanzo gently brushes his lips against mine. The kiss is tender and filled with an unspoken promise, as if our souls are intertwining in that single moment. The world around us fades into the background, and all that matters is the warmth of his touch and the depth of our connection.

We pull away, our eyes locked, and a knowing smile graces Llanzo's face. "Keisha, this sunset is just the beginning. It's a reminder that our love story is still unfolding, and there are countless chapters of adventures and shared moments waiting for us."

I nod, my heart brimming with anticipation. "Yes, Llanzo. Together, we'll embrace every sunrise and sunset, every twist and turn that life brings our way. Our love is a journey, and I can't wait to see where it leads us."

We sit there, hand in hand, as the sun dips below the horizon, painting the sky with a final burst of color. The world is now cast in the ethereal hues of twilight, and a blanket of stars emerges, sparkling above us like diamonds in the night.

In that moment, surrounded by the beauty of nature and the depth of our love, I feel a sense of peace and contentment. The universe seems to align itself perfectly, as if it's whispering its approval of the love we've found in each other.

As we rise from the beach, our footsteps leaving imprints in the sand, I know that this chapter of our Jamaican adventure is drawing to a close. But with each step we take, I am filled with excitement for the chapters yet to come, for the stories we'll create together, and for the love that will continue to blossom and thrive.

Hand in hand, we make our way back to the resort, our hearts filled with a newfound certainty and an unbreakable bond. The night is still young, and our souls are intertwined in a love that knows no boundaries.

As the day draws to a close, we find ourselves perched atop a cliff overlooking the turquoise sea. The setting sun paints the sky in a breathtaking array of pinks and oranges, casting a golden glow over our surroundings. We sit in quiet contemplation, our hearts overflowing with gratitude for this shared adventure.

I realize that our journey in Jamaica has become a metaphor for our budding relationship. We have traversed through hidden paths, explored uncharted territories, and discovered the beauty that lies within each other. Together, we have created memories that will forever be etched in the fabric of our love story.

As the sky transforms into a canvas of stars, we wrap our arms around each other, finding solace in the warmth of our embrace. We exchange whispered promises, vows to continue embarking on countless adventures together, both in Jamaica and beyond.

In the embrace of this Jamaican adventure, I am filled with a sense of profound gratitude for the serendipitous path that brought us together. The love that blossoms between us feels as boundless as the vast expanse of the Jamaican landscape. As we watch the moon rise over the horizon, its gentle glow illuminates our souls, intertwining our destinies in a tapestry of shared dreams and unwavering devotion.

We have embraced the thrill of exploration, both within the captivating landscapes and within the depths of our hearts. Each step we take, each moment we share, further solidifies the bond that has grown between us. With each passing day, I am filled with a sense of awe at the depth of connection we have forged, a connection that transcends time and place.

As I lay in bed, the echoes of our laughter and the tender touch of our shared moments dance through my mind. I am filled with anticipation for the chapters that await us beyond this tropical paradise. Together, we will navigate the journey of life, embracing the unknown with open hearts and unwavering trust.

With a contented sigh, I close my eyes, allowing the gentle lullaby of the ocean waves to serenade me into a peaceful slumber. Tomorrow may bring new adventures, new challenges, and new horizons, but one thing remains certain—our love, kindled amidst the beauty of Jamaica, will continue to blossom and thrive, defying distance and time.

And as the sun rises on a new day, casting its golden rays over the world, I wake up with a heart brimming with gratitude for the love we have found in each other. Our Jamaican adventure may be coming to an end, but the love it has ignited will endure, a flame that will guide us through the chapters that lie ahead, painting our lives with the vibrant hues of passion, companionship, and unwavering devotion.

Facing Reality

❧

Kiesha

As I sit on the balcony of my beachfront bungalow, a sense of bittersweetness washes over me. The warm Jamaican breeze carries with it a reminder that my sabbatical is drawing to a close. It's been two months of soul-stirring adventures, heartwarming connections, and falling in love with both the island and a remarkable man named.

I take a sip of my freshly brewed coffee, savoring the rich flavors as I watch the sun rise over the turquoise waters. The vibrant hues of orange and pink paint the sky, casting a mesmerizing glow on the landscape. Jamaica has been my sanctuary, a place where I found solace, healing, and a renewed sense of purpose.

But as the days have turned into weeks, and the weeks into months, reality has slowly crept in. Soon, I'll have to bid farewell to the tranquil shores, the vibrant culture, and the warmth of the Jamaican people. I'll have to leave behind the memories we've created, the laughter we've shared, and the love that has blossomed between Llanzo and me.

The thought of leaving tugs at my heart, like an invisible force gently pulling me back to the life I had left behind. The life of deadlines, investigations, and the relentless pursuit of stories. It's a life that I had grown weary of, leading me to embark on this sabbatical in the first place. But now, as my time in Jamaica nears its end, I find myself torn between the paradise I've discovered and the responsibilities awaiting me back home.

I gaze out at the sprawling palm trees swaying in the breeze, their leaves whispering secrets in the wind. Memories of our adventures flood my mind — snorkeling in crystal-clear waters, hiking through lush rainforests, and dancing to the rhythm of reggae music under the starlit sky. Each experience has left an indelible mark on my soul, reminding me of the vibrant spirit of this island and the freedom I've found in embracing life's simple pleasures.

And then there's Llanzo, the man who has woven himself into the fabric of my being. His warm smile, his infectious laughter, and the way his eyes light up when he talks about his beloved Jamaica — all of it has captivated me from the moment we met. We've shared moments of vulnerability, laughter, and deep connection that I never thought possible. The love that has blossomed between us is undeniable, but the impending departure hangs like a shadow over our hearts.

As the days dwindle down, we've been cherishing every stolen moment, every shared glance that speaks volumes, and every touch that ignites a spark within us. We both know that our time together is limited, and yet we refuse to let the looming goodbye dampen our spirits. Instead, we choose to live in the present, savoring each precious second as if it were an eternity.

But as the sun climbs higher in the sky, casting its golden rays on the pristine white sand, reality comes crashing back. I know that soon I'll have to pack my bags, board a plane, and return to the life I had momentarily escaped. It's a reality that fills me with a sense of longing and uncertainty.

Yet, amidst the whirlwind of emotions, there is a glimmer of hope. The hope that our paths will cross again, that destiny will bring us together once more. We've forged a connection that defies distance and time, and I believe in the power of our love to transcend the boundaries that separate us.

So, as I take one last sip of coffee, I make a silent vow to carry this Jamaican paradise within me, forever etched in my heart. I will treasure the memories and the profound impact this journey has had on my soul. I'll carry the warmth of the Jamaican sun, the rhythm of the reggae beats, and the taste of saltwater on my lips wherever I go. Though my sabbatical may be coming to an end soon, the spirit of adventure, love, and self-discovery will remain alive within me. I find solace in the knowledge that Jamaica will always hold a special place in my heart. The experiences I've had, the people I've met, and the love I've found have forever changed me.

With a heavy heart and a grateful soul, I step out onto the balcony, taking in the breathtaking view before me. The vast expanse of the ocean stretches out, merging with the horizon, as if whispering promises of new beginnings and reunions yet to come. And as I close my eyes, I carry with me the belief that love knows no boundaries, and that the memories we've created in this Jamaican paradise will forever live on in our hearts.

Goodbye

Keisha

As my sabbatical in Jamaica comes to an end, a mixture of emotions washes over me. Excitement for the adventures that await me back home mingles with a tinge of sadness for leaving behind the place where our love blossomed. Llanzo and I have spent incredible moments together, creating memories that will forever hold a special place in my heart.

We find ourselves sitting on a secluded beach, the waves gently lapping at the shore. The sun begins its descent, casting a warm golden glow across the horizon. I feel a knot tightening in my chest, knowing that soon I'll have to board the plane and leave this paradise behind. Tears threaten to spill from my eyes, but I try to hold them back, not wanting to spoil our final moments together.

Llanzo senses my inner turmoil, his hand reaching out to gently grasp mine. His touch brings me comfort, and I turn to look into his eyes, searching for solace. "Keisha," he says softly, his voice filled with tenderness, "I want you to know how much these past weeks have meant to me. Being with you has been a gift, and I cherish every moment we've shared."

A single tear escapes my eye, and Llanzo wipes it away with his thumb. I take a deep breath, trying to steady my trembling voice. "Llanzo, I can't deny the impact you've had on my life. This sabbatical was meant to be a break, a time for me to relax and recharge. But it became so much more. You became so much more."

He pulls me closer, wrapping his arms around me in a comforting embrace. "Keisha, I can't imagine my life without you. From the moment we met, I felt a connection unlike anything I've ever experienced. You've awakened something in me, something I thought was lost forever."

I lean into his embrace, feeling the strength of his love enveloping me. "But Llanzo, we both know that I have to go back home. My work, my responsibilities, they're waiting for me.

He looks into my eyes, his gaze filled with determination. "Keisha, distance may separate us physically, but it won't diminish the love we share. We can make this work, Keisha. We can navigate the challenges that come our way. I'm willing to do whatever it takes."

Tears stream down my face now, a mix of sadness and overwhelming love. "Llanzo, I want to believe in us. I want to believe that our love can withstand the test of time and distance. But it won't be easy. There will be moments of longing, of missing each other fiercely."

He brushes a strand of hair away from my face, his touch gentle and reassuring. "I know it won't be easy, Keisha. But our love is worth fighting for. We can use technology to bridge the gap between us, to stay connected despite the miles. We can make plans to visit each other, to create new memories in different places. And in the end, when we're finally together again, it will be all the more sweeter."

I take a deep breath, my heart pounding with a mix of fear and hope. "Llanzo, I love you. I love you with every fiber of my being. And I'm willing to take this leap of faith, to see where our love takes us."

He smiles, his eyes shining with love and determination. "Keisha, I love you too, more than words can express. And I promise you, no matter the distance, no matter the obstacles, I will always be here for you. We'll face this journey together, hand in hand."

We hold each other tightly, our hearts beating as one. In that moment, I feel a sense of peace and certainty wash over me. Despite the challenges ahead, I know that our love is resilient and that we have the strength to overcome any obstacle.

As the sun sets on our time in Jamaica, we make a promise to each other. We vow to communicate every day, to share our joys and sorrows, to support and uplift one another from afar. We make plans for future visits, for exploring new destinations together, and for creating new memories that will add to the tapestry of our love story.

The sound of the crashing waves serves as a backdrop to our conversation, a reminder of the vastness of the world and the infinite possibilities that lie ahead. We speak of dreams and aspirations, of building a future together, and the excitement in Llanzo's eyes mirrors my own.

As the night deepens, we sit on the beach, gazing at the starry sky above. Hand in hand, we make promises to each other, promises of trust, loyalty, and unwavering love. Our souls are intertwined, and no matter the distance, we know that our hearts will always be connected.

With a sense of bittersweetness, we rise from the sand and begin our walk back to the resort. The moon casts a soft glow, illuminating our path and guiding us forward. It is a symbol of hope, reminding us that love knows no boundaries, that it can transcend time and space.

At the door of my room, we linger for a moment, reluctant to say goodbye. Llanzo brushes a gentle kiss on my forehead, his touch imbued with tenderness and longing. "Until we meet again, my love," he whispers, his voice filled with both sadness and hope.

I smile through tears, feeling the depth of his words. "Until then, my heart belongs to you, Llanzo. No matter where we are, know that you are always with me."

With one last lingering look, we part ways, carrying the essence of our love with us. As I lay in bed that night, thoughts of Llanzo fill my mind. I am filled with gratitude for the time we shared, the love we discovered, and the promise of a future together.

And as I drift off to sleep, I hold onto the belief that love knows no boundaries, and that no matter the distance, our hearts will always find their way back to each other.

Keisha Returns to Miami

Keisha

As I step off the plane and set foot back in Miami, my heart feels heavy with both longing and anticipation. Thoughts of Llanzo flood my mind, his smile etched in my memory, his voice echoing in my ears. I can still feel the warmth of his touch and the way his presence brought a sense of calm and joy to my soul.

The days that follow are a whirlwind of emotions. I settle back into my routine, but my mind is constantly drifting back to our time together in Jamaica. The phone becomes my lifeline, connecting me to Llanzo across the miles. We spend hours on video calls, sharing our stories, our laughter, and our dreams. The screen may separate us physically, but our hearts remain intertwined.

Returning to work proves to be more challenging than I anticipated. The familiar stress of deadlines and demanding assignments creeps back into my life, and I find myself longing for the simplicity and serenity of the Jamaican shores. The contrast between the vibrant island life and the bustling cityscape of Miami is stark, and I yearn for the tranquility that Llanzo brought into my days.

During our daily conversations, we talk about everything and nothing at the same time. We share the mundane details of our lives, the little triumphs and setbacks, and yet every conversation is laced with an underlying current of longing and desire. We talk about the future, about the possibility of a life together, and the thought fills me with both excitement and trepidation.

The distance between us weighs heavily on my heart. I find myself yearning for his touch, for the way his presence made me feel alive and cherished. Each night, as I lay in bed, I close my eyes and imagine him beside me, his arms wrapped around me, his lips brushing against mine. The virtual connection we have sustains me, but it is no substitute for the physical closeness we shared.

As the days turn into weeks, I find solace in our nightly rituals. We create our own little world through the screen, sharing virtual meals, watching movies together, and even going on virtual walks. The moments of laughter and intimacy we share bridge the gap between us, reminding me that our love knows no boundaries.

But amidst the love and longing, there are moments of doubt and fear. The challenges of a long-distance relationship loom before us, and I question if we can withstand the test of time and distance. Self-doubt creeps in, whispering uncertainties and insecurities. Will our connection remain strong? Can our love thrive amidst the challenges that lie ahead?

Yet, in the depths of my heart, I know that love is worth

fighting for. Our bond is built on a foundation of trust, understanding, and shared experiences. It is in the way Llanzo listens, the way he supports me through the highs and lows, that I find strength. Together, we navigate the uncertainties, reassuring each other that our love is steadfast and unwavering.

Each day brings us closer to the next time we will be together. We count down the days, eagerly anticipating the moment when we can finally bridge the physical distance and be in each other's arms once again. And in those moments, I find solace and hope.

As I navigate my days in Miami, I hold onto the memories we created in Jamaica. They sustain me and remind me of the love we share. The ocean breeze, the warmth of the sun, and the echoes of our laughter linger in my mind, offering a respite from the daily grind.

And as I look ahead to the future, I am filled with both excitement and a tinge of apprehension. The road may be long and challenging, but I know that love has the power to conquer all obstacles. Our love story is not without its obstacles, but I am determined to face them head-on. The distance may be daunting, but I refuse to let it define the course of our relationship. We make plans for visits, setting dates on the calendar to ensure that our time together becomes a reality.

In the midst of the daily grind, I find solace in the thought of our shared future. Llanzo's unwavering support and encouragement fuel my determination to pursue my dreams while nurturing our love. We discuss the possibilities of my career, exploring ways in which I can continue to write and investigate while also fostering our relationship.

The challenges of a long-distance relationship become opportunities for growth and resilience. We learn to communicate even more deeply, to express our desires, fears, and vulnerabilities. Each day, we uncover new layers of trust and understanding, building a foundation that strengthens our bond.

While the physical distance may keep us apart, technology becomes our ally. We bridge the gap through phone calls, video chats, and messages that traverse the miles in an instant. Our screens become portals, connecting our hearts and souls, reminding us that love knows no boundaries.

And amidst the challenges and uncertainties, there is a constant flame of hope burning within us. We hold onto the memories of our time together, the laughter, the shared adventures, and the moments of pure bliss. Those memories become the fuel that propels us forward, reminding us of the depth and beauty of our love.

As the days turn into weeks and the weeks into months, I grow more certain of our connection. The distance may test our patience, but it also reinforces the strength of our commitment. We create rituals, small gestures of love that transcend the miles. A handwritten letter arrives in my mailbox, carrying Llanzo's words of affection. Care packages filled with tokens of his love find their way to my doorstep, reminding me that he is always with me, even when physically apart.

The support of our loved ones becomes an anchor in this journey. Friends and family who witness the depth of our love rally around us, offering encouragement and reassurance. Their words of wisdom and understanding remind me that I am not alone in this path. Together, we navigate the complexities of a long-distance relationship, knowing that our love is worth the temporary sacrifices.

And so, as I go about my days in Miami, I carry Llanzo with me in my heart. His presence is felt in the little moments, the mundane routines, and the quiet spaces. The love we share permeates every aspect of my life, infusing it with a sense of purpose and fulfillment.

As the sun sets over the city, I find comfort in the knowledge that our love is resilient, transcending the physical distance between us. We continue to nurture our connection, cherishing the moments of togetherness and eagerly awaiting the next opportunity to be in each other's arms.

And as I lay in bed each night, I close my eyes and visualize a future where the distance fades away, where we are no longer separated by miles and time zones. I envision a life where we can wake up to each other's smiles, where our laughter echoes through the hallways of a shared home.

For now, we hold onto the promise of love, knowing that it will guide us through this chapter of our lives. With each passing day, our bond grows stronger, reaffirming our belief that true love can overcome any obstacle.

And so, I embrace the challenges of a long-distance relationship, knowing that the reward is a love that defies boundaries. As I navigate the uncertainties of the present, I am filled with hope and excitement for the future we will create together, a future where distance is a mere memory, and our love reigns supreme.

Surprise Visit

~⚬⚬⚬~

Llanzo

As I step off the plane in Miami, a surge of excitement courses through my veins. I can hardly contain the smile that spreads across my face, knowing that I am about to surprise Keisha with a visit. Four months have passed since we last held each other in our arms, and the longing to be with her has only intensified with time.

I hail a taxi and give the driver the address to Keisha's apartment. As we navigate through the streets of Miami, memories of our time together flood my mind. The vibrant cityscape seems to mirror the energy and vibrancy that Keisha embodies. I can't help but feel a sense of anticipation building within me as we draw closer to our reunion.

When we arrive at her apartment building, I pay the driver and step out onto the bustling sidewalk. Taking a deep breath, I make my way towards the entrance, my heart pounding with a mix of nerves and excitement. I reach for the small box in my pocket, the surprise I have been planning for weeks, and take a moment to compose myself before pressing the buzzer.

A familiar voice crackles through the intercom, filled with curiosity and surprise. "Hello?" Keisha's voice rings out, and I can sense a hint of excitement tinged with confusion. "Who is it?"

"It's me, Llanzo," I reply, unable to contain the excitement in my voice. "Open the door, love."

Seconds later, the door swings open, revealing Keisha standing there, her eyes widening in disbelief. She gasps, her hand flying to her mouth as she takes in the sight of me standing before her. The look of surprise and joy on her face is worth every moment of planning and anticipation.

"Llanzo!" she exclaims, her voice filled with elation. "What are you doing here?"

I step forward, closing the gap between us, and pull her into a tight embrace. The familiar scent of her hair fills my senses, and I can feel her heart beating against mine. "I couldn't stay away any longer," I whisper, my voice filled with sincerity. "I missed you, Keisha. I needed to be here with you."

Tears glisten in her eyes as she pulls away slightly, her hands cupping my face. "I can't believe you're here," she says, her voice filled with a mixture of happiness and disbelief. "I missed you too,

We stand there, locked in each other's gaze, the world around us fading into the background. In that moment, nothing else matters but the love and connection we share. We spend hours catching up, sharing stories of our time apart, and relishing in the simple joy of being together again.

As the evening unfolds, we find ourselves entwined on Keisha's couch, our fingers intertwined as we delve into the depths of our emotions. The air is charged with a palpable desire, our bodies drawn to each other in a magnetic pull. It is a moment of pure intimacy, where words become unnecessary, and our bodies speak a language only we understand.

I lean in, my lips brushing against hers in a gentle caress. It is a tender kiss, filled with the longing and passion that has built up over the months of separation. Our lips move in sync, dancing to a rhythm that only we can hear. It is a kiss that ignites a fire within us, a flame that burns with intensity.

As our kisses deepen, the room fills with a symphony of sighs and whispers, each touch and caress fueling our desire. Our hands explore familiar territory, tracing the contours of each other's bodies with a newfound hunger. Time seems to stand still as we lose ourselves in the moment, surrendering to the overwhelming sensations that consume us.

The hours blend into one another as our bodies entwine in a passionate dance. We explore every inch of each other, our hands mapping the landscape of desire, and our whispers of longing filling the air. The room becomes a sanctuary of pleasure, our connection deepening with each intimate touch.

As the night gives way to dawn, we find ourselves wrapped in each other's arms, basking in the afterglow of our love. The world outside ceases to exist as we lie there, our bodies intertwined, our hearts beating in synchrony. It is in these quiet moments that I realize the depth of my feelings for Keisha. She has become the anchor that grounds me, the light that illuminates my path.

* * *

Days turn into nights, and we continue to explore the depths of our connection. We take long walks along the Miami shoreline, hand in hand, sharing dreams and aspirations. We laugh, we play, we simply revel in each other's presence, savoring every precious moment.

* * *

As the weekend draws to a close, the reality of our separation looms on the horizon. We sit together, our bodies still entwined, as we discuss the future and the challenges that lie ahead. We acknowledge the distance that separates us and the obstacles we may face, but we are determined to overcome them.

"I don't want to let you go," I confess, my voice filled with a mix of vulnerability and determination. "These days with you have been nothing short of magical, Keisha. I can't imagine my life without you."

Keisha's eyes glisten with unshed tears as she nods, her fingers tracing patterns on my chest. "I feel the same way, Llanzo," she murmurs softly. "Being with you has been a revelation. I want to give us a chance, to see where this connection takes us."

We make a pact to defy the odds, to bridge the distance between us with love and commitment. We promise to communicate regularly, to make time for each other despite the challenges of our respective lives. It is a promise forged in the fires of passion and fueled by the depth of our emotions.

* * *

As the sun sets on the fourth day, I reluctantly prepare to leave. Keisha walks me to the door, her eyes filled with a mixture of sadness and hope. We stand there, holding each other tightly, as if trying to capture this moment in time.

"I'll miss you, Llanzo," she whispers, her voice filled with an undercurrent of longing.

"I'll miss you too, Keisha," I reply, my voice tinged with a hint of melancholy. "But I promise you, this is not the end. It is just the beginning of our journey together."

With one final kiss, filled with a bittersweet mixture of love and longing, I step out into the Miami night, my heart heavy with the ache of separation. But as I make my way back to Jamaica, a newfound sense of hope and determination fills my soul. Our love will endure, transcending time and distance, for it is a love worth fighting for.

And so, as I gaze out of the airplane window, watching the lights of Miami fade into the distance, I carry with me the memory of our time together, the warmth of our embrace, and the unwavering belief that love knows no boundaries.

The Move

Keisha

The days since Llanzo's departure have been a blur of mundane routines and overwhelming work responsibilities. Each passing day feels like an eternity as I try to navigate through the demands of my job, but my heart remains heavy with the absence of Llanzo. The stress of work has once again taken its toll on me, leaving me feeling drained and unfulfilled.

I find myself constantly daydreaming, my thoughts drifting back to the moments we shared, the warmth of his embrace, and the genuine connection we forged. Memories of our time together become a lifeline, offering solace and respite from the chaotic world around me. The mere thought of Llanzo brings a smile to my face, a glimmer of hope amidst the turmoil.

As the weeks turn into months, the longing intensifies, and the realization dawns upon me that a mere phone call or video chat is no longer enough. I yearn for his touch, his presence, and the way he effortlessly puts my mind at ease. The distance between us has become unbearable, and I can no longer deny the depths of my feelings for him.

Work, once a source of purpose and fulfillment, now feels like an endless cycle of stress and exhaustion. The weight of deadlines and expectations hangs heavily upon my shoulders, suffocating any sense of joy or passion. It becomes clear to me that something has to change, that I can no longer sacrifice my happiness and well-being for the sake of a demanding career.

* * *

And so, after months of contemplation and soul-searching, I make the courageous decision to follow my heart and embark on a journey to Montego Bay. It is a leap of faith, a declaration of love and commitment, as I choose to prioritize my own happiness and pursue a life intertwined with Llanzo.

The decision is not without its challenges and doubts. Leaving behind the familiar comforts of home and taking a leap into the unknown is both exhilarating and terrifying. But the love that Llanzo and I share, the connection that has transcended time and distance, gives me the strength to face the uncertainty.

* * *

As I board the plane bound for Montego Bay, a mixture of excitement and nervous anticipation fills my being. The familiar sights and sounds of the city welcome me with open arms, as if the universe is conspiring to bring us together. The weight of work-related stress slowly lifts off my shoulders, replaced by a renewed sense of purpose and adventure.

Upon landing, I am greeted by the warm tropical breeze and the vibrant colors of Jamaica. The air feels charged with possibility, as if every step I take brings me closer to the love I have traveled so far to find. And as I make my way to Llanzo's waiting arms, a wave of peace washes over me, reaffirming the rightness of my decision.

Together, Llanzo and I embark on a new chapter of our lives, guided by love, trust, and a shared vision for the future. The days blend into a beautiful tapestry of exploration and togetherness, as we immerse ourselves in the wonders of Montego Bay. We stroll hand in hand along pristine beaches, savor the flavors of local cuisine, and dance under the moonlit skies.

The stresses that once consumed my existence fade into insignificance, replaced by the joy and contentment that come from being with the person who completes me. Llanzo's presence is a balm to my weary soul, and his unwavering support fuels my determination to create a life filled with love, happiness, and fulfillment.

As I look into his eyes, I see a reflection of my own dreams and desires. We make plans, set goals, and envision a future where our love knows no bounds. The long distance that once separated us is now The long distance that once separated us is now a distant memory, replaced by the intimacy and closeness we share in the present moment. Our days are filled with laughter, adventure, and the effortless ease that comes from being in each other's company.

With Llanzo by my side, I rediscover the beauty of Montego Bay through his eyes. He becomes my guide, showing me hidden gems and secret spots that only a local would know. We explore breathtaking waterfalls, hike through lush rainforests, and indulge in the vibrant culture that surrounds us.

Amidst the natural wonders that unfold before us, our conversations delve into deeper realms. We speak of our hopes, dreams, and fears, sharing our vulnerabilities and trusting each other with our most intimate thoughts. Llanzo's wisdom and perspective enrich my own understanding of life, and his unwavering belief in me gives me the strength to overcome any obstacles that come our way.

But it is in the quiet moments, when the sun sets and paints the sky with hues of gold and pink, that our connection truly deepens. As we sit on the beach, our bodies entwined, we bask in the serenity of the ocean's melody. Words become unnecessary, as our hearts communicate in a language only love understands.

It is during one such magical evening that our love blossoms into something even more profound. As the stars illuminate the night sky, Llanzo takes my hand, his touch igniting a spark that reverberates through every fiber of my being. The world around us fades into insignificance, and in that moment, there is only us, consumed by the sheer intensity of our love.

With tender kisses and gentle caresses, we surrender to the depth of our desires. Our bodies intertwine in a passionate dance, each touch a testament to the unspoken promises we make to each other. Time ceases to exist as we explore the depths of physical and emotional connection, savoring every moment as if it were our last.

In the afterglow of our lovemaking, we lie entwined, our breaths slowing, our hearts beating in synchrony. Llanzo's arms provide solace and security, wrapping around me with a tenderness that speaks volumes. We exchange whispered declarations of love, promising to cherish and nurture what we have found in each other.

* * *

As the days pass, our bond grows stronger. We navigate the challenges of daily life together, supporting each other through the ups and downs with unwavering devotion. The distance that once plagued us becomes insignificant, for our love transcends physical barriers and defies the limitations of time.

And so, in this idyllic paradise of Montego Bay, we lay the foundation for a future built on love, trust, and unwavering commitment. With every passing day, our love story unfolds, a testament to the power of following our hearts and taking risks in the pursuit of true happiness.

As we embrace the sun-kissed shores and breathe in the sweet scent of the Caribbean breeze, we know deep within our souls that this is where we are meant to be. Together, we create a sanctuary of love, a haven where our spirits can soar, and where our love will continue to flourish, undeterred by any distance or obstacle that may come our way.

Happily Ever After Mon

Keisha

One Year Later....

I stand there on the beach, the soft sand beneath my feet, as Llanzo takes my hand in his. The sun casts a warm glow across the horizon, painting the sky in shades of pink and orange. My heart flutters with anticipation, sensing that something special is about to happen.

Llanzo looks into my eyes, his gaze filled with love and determination. His voice trembles slightly as he begins to speak. "Keisha, from the moment we met, you've brought so much light and happiness into my life. You've shown me what it means to love and be loved, and I can't imagine my life without you."

My breath catches in my throat, my heart pounding in my chest. I can hardly believe what I'm hearing. Llanzo continues, his words carrying a depth of emotion that touches my soul. "Keisha, will you marry me? Will you spend the rest of your life with me, creating a lifetime of beautiful memories together?"

Tears well up in my eyes as I nod, unable to find my voice amidst the overwhelming joy and love that fills my heart. Llanzo takes a small velvet box from his pocket and opens it, revealing a stunning diamond ring. He slides it onto my finger, and in that moment, it feels as if our souls have intertwined, bound together by an unbreakable love.

As the waves crash against the shore, we hold each other tightly, our embrace a testament to the depth of our connection. I whisper my heartfelt "Yes" into his ear, the words carrying a world of promises and dreams.

We stand there, basking in the glow of the setting sun, feeling the weight of this profound moment. Llanzo's smile lights up his face, and I can see the sheer happiness radiating from him. In this instant, I know that we have embarked on a new chapter of our lives, one filled with love, companionship, and a shared vision for the future.

Our hearts are filled with an overwhelming sense of gratitude and excitement. We talk for hours, envisioning our wedding day, discussing our hopes and dreams, and the life we want to build together. The beach becomes a canvas upon which we paint a picture of our future, filled with laughter, adventure, and a love that knows no bounds.

As we hold hands, I can't help but feel an incredible sense of peace and contentment. The world around us fades into the background as we focus on this moment, this turning point in our lives. We are no longer just two individuals, but a team, ready to face life's challenges together, and celebrate its joys as one.

In that magical moment on the beach, Llanzo's proposal becomes a cherished memory, etched into the fabric of our love story. It is a testament to the power of love, the beauty of connection, and the infinite possibilities that lie ahead. As we walk hand in hand along the shoreline, the future shimmers with promise, and I am filled with gratitude for the love we share and the adventure that awaits us.

* * *

Eight Months Later...

As I stand on the pristine sandy beach, the sun casting its golden glow on the turquoise waters, I reflect on the incredible journey that has led me to this moment. It has been a year since I made the life-changing decision to move to Montego Bay and be with the love of my life, Llanzo. And now, as I feel the warm embrace of the ocean breeze, I am filled with a profound sense of joy and anticipation for what the future holds.

It was just a few weeks ago when Llanzo took me by surprise, dropping to one knee and presenting me with a shimmering diamond ring. The proposal was everything I had ever dreamed of - intimate, heartfelt, and filled with the depth of his love for me. With tears of joy streaming down my face, I said yes without hesitation, knowing in my heart that I had found my soulmate.

And so, on this glorious day, we stand before our closest family and friends, the gentle sound of waves serving as our symphony. The beach is adorned with vibrant tropical flowers, their vibrant colors reflecting the beauty of our love. As I walk down the aisle, my heart flutters with excitement, my eyes locked with Llanzo's, who stands at the altar, his expression a perfect blend of love and adoration.

The ceremony is a testament to our love, with heartfelt vows exchanged, promising to love, cherish, and support each other through the ups and downs of life. The words we speak carry weight and meaning, sealing our commitment in the presence of those who have been witness to our journey. The sun begins its descent, casting a warm glow over us, as we exchange rings, symbolizing the eternal bond we share.

As I stand before Llanzo, our hands clasped together, and the pastor standing beside us, I take a deep breath, feeling a mixture of nerves and overwhelming love. This is the moment we've been waiting for, the moment when we exchange our vows and commit our lives to one another. The sound of the ocean waves crashing against the shore provides a soothing backdrop to this sacred moment.

The pastor looks at us with a warm smile, and I can see the sincerity in his eyes. He begins the ceremony, inviting us to share our vows. Llanzo's gaze meets mine, and I can feel the depth of his love and devotion.

"Llanzo," I begin, my voice trembling slightly with emotion, "from the first moment we met, you captured my heart in a way I never thought possible. You've shown me a love that is pure, unwavering, and unconditional. Today, I stand before you, ready to make a vow that will last a lifetime."

I take a moment to compose myself, the weight of my words sinking in. "I promise to stand by your side, through all the ups and downs that life may bring. I promise to support you, encourage you, and uplift you in all your endeavors. I promise to be your rock, your confidante, and your best friend. I promise to love you fiercely, with every beat of my heart, and to cherish our bond with gratitude and joy."

Llanzo's eyes glisten with tears of happiness as he takes his turn to speak his vows. His voice is filled with emotion, and I hang onto every word he utters.

"Keisha," he says, his voice steady yet filled with intensity, "you are the light that brightens my days, the warmth that fills my heart. You've shown me what it means to truly love and be loved. Today, I stand here before you, humbled and grateful for the gift of your love."

He pauses, taking a deep breath, and continues, "I promise to honor and respect you, to be your partner in all aspects of life. I promise to listen to you with an open heart, to support you in your dreams and aspirations. I promise to be there for you, through thick and thin, and to always hold your hand as we navigate life's journey together. I promise to love you unconditionally, to laugh with you, and to be your safe haven in times of darkness."

As Llanzo finishes his vows, I am overcome with a flood of emotions. Our vows encapsulate the love, commitment, and promises we make to one another, setting the foundation for a lifetime of happiness and devotion.

The pastor smiles warmly at us, his eyes reflecting the love and joy that surrounds us. He speaks words of wisdom and guidance, reminding us of the sacredness of marriage and the importance of nurturing our bond.

In that moment, as we exchange rings and declare our love for all to witness, I feel an overwhelming sense of gratitude and bliss. We seal our vows with a tender kiss, surrounded by the embrace of our loved ones and the beauty of the ocean backdrop.

As the ceremony concludes and we begin our journey as husband and wife, I am filled with an indescribable sense of joy. Our vows are not just words, but a testament to the love we share, a love that will continue to grow and thrive as we embark on this beautiful chapter of our lives.

As the evening progresses, laughter and joy fill the air. We dance under the starry sky, our bodies swaying to the rhythm of love. The sound of laughter and the clinking of glasses echo throughout the night, celebrating our union and the beginning of a new chapter in our lives.

* * *

Five Months Later...

Months pass, and the love between Llanzo and me continues to deepen and flourish. And then, on a sunny afternoon, a feeling of both excitement and nervousness envelops me as I hold the pregnancy test in my trembling hands. The positive result confirms what my heart already knows - we are about to embark on the journey of parenthood.

With a mixture of awe and wonder, Llanzo and I embrace the news, our hearts overflowing with joy. We dream of the life growing within me, imagining the adventures, love, and laughter that will fill our home. We eagerly share the news with our families, who are overjoyed at the prospect of welcoming a new member into our close-knit circle.

Together, we prepare for the arrival of our little one, creating a nurturing and loving environment. We paint the nursery with soft pastel hues, carefully selecting every detail to create a haven of comfort and warmth. Llanzo's hands tenderly caress my growing belly, feeling the gentle kicks and movements that serve as a constant reminder of the miracle of life.

* * *

As the days turn into weeks, and the weeks into months, we eagerly anticipate the arrival of our bundle of joy. We attend birthing classes, read parenting books, and surround ourselves with the support of friends and family. Our love for each other and our growing baby strengthens, creating a solid foundation of love and security.

And so, as I stand here, hand in hand with Llanzo, gazing into the horizon, I am filled with a deep sense of gratitude for the incredible journey we have embarked upon. The challenges we have faced and the triumphs we have celebrated have only served to deepen our love and commitment to each other.

As we look forward to the future, our hearts overflow with excitement and anticipation. We imagine the joy of holding our baby in our arms, the sleepless nights filled with tender moments and soothing lullabies. We envision family outings, beach strolls with tiny feet leaving imprints in the sand, and the laughter that will fill our home.

* * *

The months pass swiftly, and soon the day arrives when our precious baby makes their grand entrance into the world. The delivery room is filled with a mix of emotions - anticipation, nervousness, and an overwhelming sense of love. Llanzo stands by my side, his unwavering support and comforting presence reassuring me every step of the way.

I sit nervously in the doctor's office, Llanzo holding my hand tightly. Our hearts race with anticipation as the doctor prepares to reveal the gender of our baby. The room is filled with a mix of excitement and nervous energy, and I can't help but feel a surge of emotions coursing through me.

The doctor smiles warmly and says, "Are you ready to find out the gender of your baby?"

I nod eagerly, my heart pounding in my chest. Llanzo and I exchange glances, our eyes filled with anticipation and love.

The doctor positions the ultrasound wand on my belly, and the screen flickers to life, revealing the precious life growing within me. As I hold my breath, the doctor maneuvers the wand, searching for the telltale sign that will reveal our baby's gender.

Suddenly, a clear image appears on the screen, and the doctor points to it, her smile widening. "Congratulations! It's a baby girl!"

A surge of joy overwhelms me, and tears well up in my eyes. A girl! I look at Llanzo, my voice choked with emotion. "We're having a girl, Llanzo! A little princess!"

Llanzo's face lights up with pure delight, his eyes sparkling with happiness. He squeezes my hand gently and whispers, "A daughter... Our daughter."

I can't contain my tears of joy as we both embrace, feeling the immense love and excitement bubbling within us. We have dreamed of this moment, of welcoming a precious little girl into our lives, and now it's becoming a reality.

The doctor offers her congratulations and provides us with more information about our baby's development. But my mind is consumed with thoughts of our baby girl. I imagine her tiny fingers and toes, her soft cries and sweet giggles. I envision the bond we will share, the memories we will create as a family.

As we leave the doctor's office, hand in hand, the world seems to glow with a newfound radiance. We talk excitedly about our daughter, discussing names and envisioning the life that awaits her. Every step feels lighter, every breath filled with anticipation.

In that moment, I feel a profound sense of gratitude for the miracle growing within me. Our daughter is a precious gift, a symbol of our love and the beautiful future that lies ahead. I know that together, as a family, we will cherish every moment, savoring the joy and wonder that comes with parenthood.

As we drive home, the sun casts a warm glow over the horizon, painting the sky with hues of pink and gold. It feels like a sign, a reminder of the little girl waiting to enter our lives. I place my hand on my belly, feeling the gentle movements of our daughter, and whisper, "We can't wait to meet you, our sweet baby girl. We love you so much already."

* * *

And then, with a cry that pierces through the room, our little one is placed in my arms. In that moment, time seems to stand still as I gaze into their innocent eyes, marveling at the miracle of life. The connection between Llanzo and me strengthens as we become parents, united by an unbreakable bond of love for our child.

* * *

Days turn into nights, and nights into weeks, as we navigate the joys and challenges of parenthood together. The sleepless nights and endless diaper changes are balanced by the pure joy and unconditional love that fills our home. Llanzo's dedication as a father is evident in every tender touch and soothing word, and I find myself falling in love with him all over again.

As our baby grows, we create a world of exploration and discovery. We embark on family adventures, introducing our little one to the breathtaking beauty of Jamaica and its rich culture. We revel in the giggles and milestones, cherishing every precious moment as time seems to slip through our fingers like grains of sand.

Our love story continues to evolve, with each passing day strengthening the foundation upon which our relationship is built. We find solace in the quiet moments, stolen kisses amidst the chaos of parenthood, and whispered promises of forever. Through the challenges that life may present, we face them hand in hand, knowing that together we can overcome anything.

And so, as I reflect on the journey that has brought us to this point, I am overwhelmed with gratitude for the love we share. Our lives are a tapestry woven with threads of joy, laughter, and unwavering support. We are a family, bound together by a love that knows no bounds.

As the sun sets on this chapter of our lives, a new one begins, filled with endless possibilities and adventures yet to come. Our love story continues to unfold, and with each passing day, our hearts grow fuller, our bond deeper, and our appreciation for the precious moments in life intensifies.

With a renewed sense of purpose, we embrace the future, knowing that as long as we have each other, we can weather any storm. Together, we will continue to build a life filled with love, laughter, and cherished memories, forever grateful for the beautiful journey that brought us to this point.

And so, with hope in our hearts and love guiding our way, we step forward into the unknown, ready to embrace the wonders that await us as a family.

About the Author

She is from a small coastal town in North Carolina and currently resides in Florida. She started reading romance novels, watching soap operas and romance/drama movies with her mother as a teenager. She then started enjoying horror, mystery, and thrillers. Her imagination and creativity started her to write her own romance novels.

Ireland started writing contemporary romance and contemporary with a little erotica and spread her wings into dark romance, reverse harem and paranormal romance.

You can connect with me on:
- https://irelandlorelei.com
- https://linktr.ee/irelandlorelei
- https://linktr.ee/irelandlorelei

Subscribe to my newsletter:

✉ https://linktr.ee/irelandlorelei

Also by Ireland Lorelei

She has written the following Series:

Seals and Bounty (7 Books) - Dark Romance

Second Chance (5 Books) - Contemporary with Erotica

Vegas Blue written in Susan Stokers World (4 Books) - Contemporary

The Powerful & Kinky Society - Dark Billionaire Series - Ongoing

She has written the following Standalone's:

Anonymous Love - Contemporary

Don't Tap Out (Part 1) & Don't Tap Out Again (Part 2) - Dark Romance

Entangled (Part 1) & UnEntangled (Part 2) - Contemporary with Erotica

From the Ashes - Dark Romance

Island Christmas - Contemporary

Just Breathe - Dark Romance

Naughty or Nice - Cuffs, Clamps & Candle Wax - Dark Romance

Secret Spark - Dark Romance

She has written in Anthologies:

Friends to Lovers; Mistletoe Kisses; Lovely Benefits; Personal Demons; Falling For My Best Friend;

She published a collection of her short stories in "Dreams Come True" and she released her first "Authors Planner" in 2022.

Masquerade Party
Book One - The Powerful & Kinky Society Series

Michael Anderson is the young billionaire bachelor who is the owner and CEO of *The Royal Grande Hotels and Resorts* and she's a new entry level marketing assistant in his marketing department. He's walked by her a hundred times in his offices and never really noticed her.

Abigail Baker is an average just out of college, entry level marketing associate at one of the biggest hotel and resort chains in the world. Her career goals are to work her way up the marketing chains to Chief Marketing Officer. She is focused and keeps her personal life and work life separate.

Abigail meets a man at a masquerade party and unbeknown to her at the time, he is the owner and CEO of the company that she works for. She never recognized him as her CEO and of course he didn't even know she existed on his payroll. By the time she realizes who he is, they have already begun to play.

He brings out her deepest sexual desires. She wants to learn more about the BDSM world and offers to teach her how to be a sub, but not just any sub, his sub.

What happens when this well-established man who is fifteen years older than her, awakens sexual desires that she never knew she had? Can they both keep their personal life and business separate? Can they keep their growing feelings for each other at bay and stick to the contract?

Raven

Raven Morgan had been brutally attacked and almost died. The man that saved her, Reggie Brown, wasn't a living man at all. He was a vampire and to save her he had to turn her and make her immortal.

On their mission to take revenge on the men that attacked her, Raven meets Reggie's only friend, Ronan Pierce who joins them in their revenge.

Once she has been avenged, the three decide to continue together to Ronan's estate in Pennsylvania and hang out for a while. But feelings start to emerge. Reggie and Ronan both are very protective of her and those feelings grow into them wanting her.

Raven tries to choose between them and then realizes that she can't choose. She wants them both.

But another battle is in their future and in walks Lucas. Can they defeat the vampire hunters? Will Lucas join the trio making them a quad?

Milton Keynes UK
Ingram Content Group UK Ltd.
UKHW032044180324
439698UK00001B/21